The Haven

J.W. Webb

Cover art by Linda Garland
Book designed by Debbi Stocco, MyBookDesigner.com

13-ISBN: 978-0-9863507-7-1 (paperback)
13-ISBN: 978-0-9565182-4-8 (digital)

The Maid of Haven

Time and tide print the lover's footstep that leads to children's castles and then are washed away. White gull echoes hue and cry and eager waves kiss slated shores safe in the knowledge that once again they will meet upon the skyline. Only then she comes to the Haven...

Silently, patiently, she rises to wait upon a tide that releases and the time that heals. Longingly she has waited; holding the scene upon this summer day so different from the wild seas that took him long ago, when tortured wind ripped her soul and left an empty life short lived. Returning with each tide, in measured moments, she awaits his call...

The unseen smile honours the beauty in each passing day and the joy of their eternal love is celebrated by her timeless duty. Tidal swell eddies at her feet and evening star welcomes night and still she alone remains to hasten his return. Not in loneliness, but in shallows keeping, The Maid of Haven waits...

~ Rae Pugh

For Rae

'Time scatters seeds to the wind
Life is but a moment flowering'

Table of Contents

Chapter 1

Sanctuary

WHAT A WAY TO SPEND a Friday night—lost in a tunnel of rain, mist and cloying dark. Richard Harrison, enduring husband and struggling optimist, now questioned his wisdom in choosing Cornwall for their weekend retreat. It had seemed adventurous back in his sitting room in Battersea—but on reflection, 'rash' was a more appropriate word. He checked his iPhone: five past eight—they'd been on the road for hours.

Richard should have known better than to suggest the West Country in November—bad decision (and not the first). Kate's mood was worsening by the mile, and this gagging sea fret was getting to him too. It had been fine when they'd turned off the A39 twenty minutes ago, but as they neared the coast, this depressing mizzle had stolen upon them, and all but swallowed their Suzuki Jimny in a dismal blanket of gloom. Richard wasn't entirely sure they were on the right lane—these corkscrew, hedge-walled ribbons of tarmac were a nightmare to navigate. They had met a milk lorry a mile back that had nearly ran them off the road, and now Kate wrenched the gear-stick as if she wanted to throttle it, her face carved in stony silence.

It was Richard's fault of course—everything was, these days. He'd suggested this trip despite Kate's reservations, and since their argument last week nothing had gone right. Richard knew things wouldn't improve until he found work again: he'd tried to explain how things were in the city these days—since the crash four years ago, it had just gotten worse. And how could he re-enter a world that had so callously cast him adrift? Twenty arse-licking years he'd laboured for the bank and, while his useless bosses got richer and fatter he, Richard (gullible idiot), had carried the can.

And then they'd fired him last winter, without so much as a 'thank you and good bye'. Kate had been sympathetic at first, but when the money stopped coming in, and she had to explain to her circle of friends (witchesandbitches.com), she had grown frostier toward him by the day.

Richard knew this weekend was their final chance; his last hope of redemption. But so far he was falling short by miles—bendy, dark and foggy miles to be exact.

"Are you certain this is the right road?" Kate rammed the stick into third: they pitched into a steep decline, the lane funnelling in close on either side until they felt smothered and cocooned. "We left the A39 ages ago," she said. "We should have reached Boscastle by now."

Kate had wanted to go to Greece for some winter sun: she didn't have a clue how broke they were. It had been hard work convincing her on this weekend West Country trip instead. She'd complied under duress, but still acted as though she resented the decision.

"It can't be far," Richard replied lamely. He felt useless—he'd offer to drive but it was Kate's car—he'd had to flog his beloved TT last year (and Kate hated anyone else driving her bloody Jimny—not that anyone with half a brain would want to commandeer such a rattling piece of crap). And to make matters worse, the satnav was playing up. Did nothing work in Cornwall? They might as well be on Mars!

Richard winced as the Suzuki screamed down the lane in third—gears weren't Kate's strong point—he squinted, winced again and then glimpsed something in the murk ahead.

"What's that?" Richard felt a glimmer of hope—just a spark. *Civilisation—at last?*

"Kate... Slow down a minute, for Christ sake."

Muttering obscenities, Kate eased back on the throttle and Richard; (still squinting,) discerned what looked to be a battered road sign, creeping out at them from the tunnel gloom ahead. He strained his eyes and focussed. 'Haven,' the sign read—or rather dripped. At last they must have reached the coast—sanctuary.

"Maybe there'll be a pub or something." Richard felt better now. "We can have a drink and look at the map again."

Kate nodded without enthusiasm, and eased the car forward to see what Haven had to offer. They were in luck. After passing a few slate-dressed houses, Richard saw a light down below. *What's that—a pub? Thank God!*

Moments later, Kate smoothly slid the Suzuki into a dimly lit car park. She turned the key, killing the engine, and took a nonce to study her tidy features in the mirror. Ahead squatted the wall of a large building, from its midst several windows spilled that welcoming light. Below these and close at hand, a shabby door hinted toward civilisation and warmth.

This will do.

They vacated the car without words. Richard stretched and yawned, then followed his neat-haired wife toward the understated entrance of what looked to be a small hotel or inn. Beyond the dripping building, the rhythmic grind of breakers heaved and sighed, and the salty brine of the Atlantic filled Richard's nostrils and eased his fretting.

Hmm... this is better... Richard took a deep breath, managed a jittery smile and then followed Kate inside.

The place was starkly furnished and rather gloomy—but at least it was clean. A lone figure sat hunched at the far end of the otherwise deserted bar, his features lugubrious and melancholy as he gazed wanly into his half-drained beer glass. Richard greeted him in friendly fashion, but the fellow just grunted and looked away. When after a moment he spoke, it was more to his beer glass than to Richard and Kate.

"There's a bell over by the till," he muttered in an accent more 'Estuary' than Cornish.

Kate wasted no time sourcing said bell. Within seconds, she'd pounced on the brass dome and thumped it three times.

Minutes passed: Kate shuffled her feet and frowned, whilst Richard looked on with forlorn hope.

Eventually a youngish freckly-faced woman poked a quizzical head through the door from the kitchen beyond.

"You wantin' lodging?" she asked, scratching an ear in indifference as she waited for their reply. Kate and Richard exchanged looks—neither desired to get back in the car again. They were both tired.

"Yep, room for two please," said Kate in her clipped Chelsea accent. "With sea views—if poss." The girl raised a brow at that. "Well it might be sunny tomorrow," Kate added tartly, while rewarding Richard with an irritated glance.

"Might be; most probably won't be," responded the girl, tucking a mousy lock behind her right ear and forcing back a yawn. She then reached across to receive Kate's charge card and swiftly rammed it into the waiting machine. "If you want anything later, I'll be at the desk. Name's Morwenna," said the girl, leaving them to settle their things in the room upstairs.

Once that was sorted, they retired to a far window in the bar lounge where, should the fret lift and the moon show his face, they would see the ocean. Richard scanned the map with interest as he downed his first pint—at least the ale was good here. Very good actually, it was a local Cornish drop from Truro he'd not come across before. The map showed that they were only a few miles from Boscastle; how they'd missed the town, Richard had no idea, but after two more excellent ales and an above average size portion of fish and chips, he was happy to soak in the atmosphere of the Haven Hotel. Boscastle would still be there in the morning.

At about ten o'clock a few locals sauntered in and took their seats, bantering in casual friendly fashion at the bar. Occasionally one would nod in the young couple's direction. Kate, in no mood for polite chit chat, retired aloft with a curt "Good night" and cold peck on Richard's cheek. Richard watched her go in thoughtful silence. He ordered another beer but when some local put the jukebox on and released the wailing tones of a recent X-Factor winner into the saloon, Richard winced and decided to take a stroll outside. It had stopped drizzling and was surprisingly mild for this late in the year.

Glass still in hand; Richard made his way through the gloom toward the luring, heaving incantation of water ahead. Above, the mist had abated just enough to reveal a pale moon rolling free from silvered cloud. It patrolled restless high above, before vanishing in the cloud again.

Richard stopped to take in the night. Ahead and to his right, a huge shoulder of rock bulked massive over what hinted to be a rocky cove. On closer inspection, Richard saw that it was a huge cliff: almost sheer—as if sliced away by a giant's knife where it met the dull glimmer of the waves.

He crossed the lane; entered the stony beach, making his way down to the water's edge two or three hundred yards ahead.

On reaching the sea, Richard stooped to wash his tired features with the cold embrace of the Atlantic. He smiled, feeling the salt cleanse his skin, and stood for a while, beer glass (empty now) swaying in left hand, just staring out into the mist that clung in vapours above the waves.

It was lifting at last. Richard could see the cove clearly now. It ran pebbly and flat for several hundred yards on either side, before rising into rocky heights that thrust seaward disappearing into the night. Richard looked forward to exploring those rocks tomorrow. He grinned, he felt better than he had for weeks; at peace with himself, as though all was as should be in his life, despite knowing blatantly otherwise.

A soft sound turned his head. Beneath the huge cliff's smothering dark Richard glimpsed the figure of someone standing, scarce yards away; watching, just as he did, the ceaseless orchestra of wave and sky.

It was a woman. She was tall: strangely clad, her long reddish hair wild as it lifted behind her in the keening sea breeze. Richard waved across to her but she seemed unaware of his presence—just continued her silent vigil of the lapping waters as they reached out toward the distant dark. Richard wondered who she was, standing so silently there. Surely she must be cold—though mild it *was* November and she wore only a dress—far as he could tell anyway. He didn't want to gape rudely at her. Or did he? For some reason this woman fascinated him. Richard wasn't a flirt and certainly was no ladies' man. But there was magnetism here and he felt intrigued. Richard, embarrassed now, coyly glanced down at his wrist-watch: half past one—he'd been out here for hours! Strange? It seemed but a few moments had passed since he'd come outside.

Tired again, Richard strolled back to the hotel, leaving the silent woman to her solitary surveillance of the waves. The car park was empty excluding Kate's Jimny and a black Golf estate lurking over in the corner. All was quiet and still in the Haven Hotel, as Richard creaked his way up the shabby stairs, and then quietly turned the door knob that opened into their room. Moonlight spilled on Kate's sleeping face as Richard clambered clumsily in beside her. Within minutes he was sound asleep.

* * *

Outside night deepens. Surge and sigh of breaker washing stone, and mournful sough of winter wind—all else silence and remoteness. The Haven sleeps: but outside others wander.

The woman watches... sees the lovers arm in arm. They have been waiting so long for this day. She knows their pain—she has lived it. They ignore her as always—there is only room for two in their world. This she understands too—having loved once long ago.

The young couple pass without a word. They are making for the sea as they always do at this hour. The tall woman watches them leave in silence. She manages a sad smile, knowing it is almost time for past and present to become one. The moon is waxing and the time now near. For some moments longer she stands there—a lonely figure framed by night, oblivious to both biting wind and salt spray's icy embrace. At last satisfied, she wanders back along the shore, her torn hem soaked and her auburn tresses tossed wild and wanton.

On she glides to ocean's arch. To her left rears the cliff-face, whilst midnight water flanks her right. She passes beneath the craggy rock just as the moon rolls free of cloud-wrack, its witchy sheen casting silver on her once so lovely face. She turns away from the ghost light and sees the others watching her nearby. The other woman's eyes are hard.

Don't interfere, those dark eyes warn her. But she has no interest in their cruel game. Hers is another place and time. She turns away, unruffled by the black-haired woman's hostile stare. Let these two work their patient, twisted game of vengeance. She has other duties—circle within a circle. It would soon be dawn and time for her to sleep. The lovers say nothing, as she fades from view in the pre-dawn glow.

Chapter 2

The Irishman

NOVEMBER 1867. DANIEL WATCHES THE girl's hips swaying, as she collects the empty plates from the tables. She catches his eye; smiles briefly, before turning and continuing with her task. Daniel winks at her and takes another sip of his malty ale. It's warm in the common room tonight and cosy, what with the huge ingle-nook fire ablaze to his left.

He'd left Ireland only last week, arriving here in Cornwall on the first step in his cajoled pilgrimage to Rome. Father Padraig had proposed the exile as penance for his 'devious indiscretions' with *that benighted woman* in Galway Town. It was bad enough that Daniel had vowed to take the priesthood, albeit unwillingly, but *said* woman being married to the local magistrate hadn't improved matters. That fine-standing gentleman (most tenaciously) had demanded that the church punish this future priest for his extreme 'reckless and irreverent' behaviour. Hence this enforced voyage to the Vatican where—Daniel's father, the priest Padraig, and everyone else he knew in County Clare and Galway Town—informed him, he was to beg mercy from the Holy Father, or at least one of his blessed cardinals.

The trouble was Daniel had never wanted to take the bloody vow; nothing against the order, but all that chastity and sanctity was not for him. That said, being in such a tight spot he'd agreed readily enough to this exile, and promised he'd return a better man—if he returned at all.

And so Daniel's enforced pilgrimage began. He owned to cheerfulness mostly, deeming things had turned out rather well. Dressed as a labourer, he'd worked passage from Cork to Bristol docks—sent word back to Clare claiming he was already half way to Rome. That was six weeks ago and Rome was a long way from Daniel's thoughts (and body) right now. Those thoughts centred wholly on laughing blue eyes and a wicked Cornish smile—the girl in the inn: Sarah.

The youngest of six brothers, there'd been little for Daniel back in the Burren. Life was lean there—especially after the bloody famine had taken its toll on the whole community. That may have been nearly twenty years ago, but times hadn't improved. Ireland was a tinderbox these days. The British Empire had done nothing to help those starving, and just six months past the Fenians had rebelled near Dublin. In Daniel's opinion, things could only get worse; the British (and Irish) landowners rode roughshod over common folk. Daniel's family were better off than most, but still he hated the injustice of it all. Three of his brothers were in America—last he heard, New York City or Boston or some such place, the remaining two were content enough with staying back home. Big Joe would inherit the farm when the old fella passed away; Kieran was alright too—having wed into money two years ago. But Daniel?

He was the black sheep that needed fencing in—hence the church impending. And so, after many harsh words and at his father's bullish insistence, Daniel had relented and vowed to take the cloth next spring.

That promise hadn't changed his nature though. He was still Danny Flannigan, idle dreamer, glib womaniser and wily charmer. *Rome could wait.*

* * *

Daniel casts an eye to the window and smiles: It is wet and dreary outside, and very dark—November was hardly the time for journeying by sea. Besides, it was warm and comfortable here.

And then there was the girl.

That girl was back again: she brushed passed his arm quickly; he caught a scent of violets, musty and sweet. Their eyes touched and laughed, his jet twinkle flirting with her dark blue mischievous orbs. He asks her name, "Sarah," she tells him—their fingers touch so very lightly and then she is gone again, off about her duties along with wink and wicked smile. Daniel smiles too: his eyes follow her retreat from the smoky room. He decides to stay put here for a while. Best not rush matters...

Throughout that whole week, Daniel lingers idle in the old coach house at Trewenny's Cross—a dusty hamlet just a few miles south of Stratton Town, where the high road meets the coastal track that winds down to Haven Cove. During his stay, Daniel writes to Father Padraig saying that he has postponed his journey south for a time so that he can do a study of Cornish saints. Padraig wouldn't be pleased, but at least he was keeping in touch and besides, he'd get to Rome eventually—there was plenty of time for that. He'd not spent all his coin—though it was thinning fast enough and he'd need to seek work in a short while.

Daniel likes Cornwall, in some ways it reminds him of home. Like Daniel's countrymen, these Cornishmen have small love for their masters, up there in London Town. They were mostly modest farming folk around these parts. But times had been hard here too and many natives had left here for Australia and other distant places.

Yes, thinks Daniel, this Cornwall is much like his home—he feels happy here, and settled. Employment was scarce in these parts though, (he'd been informed he'd find quarry work up on the moor, or else he could fare across to Port Gaverne where they exported the slate overseas.) Aside from that, Daniel could work on the railways or labour on a farm. He'd find something when needs must. But Daniel is in no urgent rush right now. He has other more pressing matters on his mind. These are swinging hips, big eyes and a wicked laughing smile—the girl, Sarah. Daniel winks at her again. *Plenty of time for work and then Rome—I'll stay put for a while yet.*

* * *

Another week passes, Daniel's warm easy manner works on both the proprietor, Big John Nichols, and his busy wife—the kindly ferret-faced Elizabeth. More importantly, Daniel also gets to know the girl, Sarah. Through those long wintry evenings they flirt effortlessly in the taproom, not caring who else watches or listens. Most ignore them and are content to smoke their pipes, drink their foggy ales, and discuss the pressing business of the day.

But there is one there that doesn't ignore them. He is Thomas Cutting, a farm labourer from nearby Treliggan Corners. During recent months Thomas has taken a proper fancy to Sarah, and even approached her on several occasions. She'd spurned his clumsy advances amid scowls. Thomas isn't popular, due to his belligerent nature. He is a big lad though, strong boned and blunt-tongued; at nineteen years stooping a head taller than anyone else in the taproom. His hair is greasy brown in hue; long in length and tied back by a shabby ribbon. The other thing about Thomas people noticed: he didn't take to bathing much.

Thomas now takes his seat two tables across from the Irishman. He covertly glares at the other man's back, whilst feigning interest in his little brother (Robert's) dull conversation.

The night deepens, the fire burns low, and people start to leave; Thomas notes the Irishman's sudden departure, and glowers hostile when he sees Sarah slip through the door leading out to the privy just a few seconds later. He seethes: after a few minutes brooding and steaming, Thomas has had enough. He gets up from his table and, ignoring Robert's quizzical glance, makes moodily for the door opening out into the stable yard and the outside privy. Thomas's cold blue eyes scan the yard until they find what they seek. He sees them there, arms entwined beneath the lamplight; Sarah's back hard against the privy door. Her blue dress is hoisted up above her knees and the Irishman is thrusting up into her with rhythmic, urgent jolts. They don't see Thomas watching, so lost are they in their passion. He watches every thrust, hears every moan— feels his calloused fists bunching nasty at his side.

When they are done, the lovers part with a brief, furtive kiss: Sarah returns flush-faced to the kitchens, and the Irishman straightens his attire before turning back toward the door.

Where Thomas accosts him.

Daniel clocks the hostile look in the big lad's eye. He'd noticed him earlier sitting with his brother—two uglier turds would be hard to imagine, so these two had to be related. The big lout looms and scowls: tries barring his way, but Daniel slips passed easily enough.

"Where's 'e going then?" Thomas growls—he's taken a deal of drink this night.

"To my bed, shortly," replies Daniel, "not that it's any of your business, yer big shite." Daniel's lips are smiling, but his eyes remain guarded and ready.

"You watch yourself, stranger," says Thomas looming over the smaller man and barring his way again. But something in Daniel's eye stops him taking it further. "I don't like you overmuch."

Daniel laughs at that. "You'll get over it, laddie, so you will. Now—if you'll excuse me, big fella." Still smiling, Daniel shoulders passed the red-faced Thomas and heads back to the taproom for a nightcap. Thomas follows behind, keeping his distance. He rejoins his brother, and together they glower into the fireplace.

Minutes later, Big John bids the smiling Irishman goodnight and Daniel retires upstairs. As he leaves the common room he notices the 'big lout' watching him. Their eyes lock, Thomas smoulders, and Daniel winks down at him. *She's not for the likes of you, big lad.*

Hours later, Thomas still sits stewing and drinking by the dwindling fire. Robert has taken his leave a half hour earlier. The room is empty now, and John the proprietor will be asking Thomas to leave at any minute. He looks up with bloodshot eyes, as beardy John looms over him.

"I'm closin' up," Big John grunts. "Drain that flagon, Thomas. Don't 'e got work in a few hours time?"

Thomas nods and yawns. "Who's that little foreign bastard and what's he doing in Trewenny's?"

"That's nay business of mine or your'n." John wipes a smear from the table. "Seems a decent enough lad—and he pays up front, unlike some other folk I could mention."

"Sarah Hosking likes him." Thomas's eyes are hooded as he looks up at John's greying bristles. "And what he was doing to her in your stable yard earlier weren't what I'd call decent."

"You know Sarah."

"Aye, I do that." Thomas drains his mug, grabs his coat, and shambles moody out the door, bulking into the gloom of the dreek November night. As he walks the three miles back to Treliggan Corners, Thomas thinks on what has occurred this evening. He decides that this Irish fellow with the smiling face and easy tongue will have to meet with an unfortunate accident—and serve the bugger right too. Nearing home, Thomas has the semblance of a plan. A cunning notion—he'd share it with Robert later. Robert would be up for it (his little brother always followed where Thomas led.) Together they'd wipe that smug grin of the stranger's face. Thomas Cutting smiles as he enters the snug glow of his cluttered cottage. The Cutting brothers would do for the Irishman soon, and then he'd be the one ploughing Sarah Hosking outside the privy at Trewenny's Cross...

Chapter 3

The Stranger

MORNING BLESSED THEM WITH A wintry sun. Kate returned from her jog to find Richard staring bleary-eyed at the mirror.

"Where'd you get to last night?" she asked him. "I woke twice and you weren't beside me."

"I went for a walk by the cliff," he replied. Kate just shrugged as she stepped in the shower. Richard could tell that she wasn't really interested. After breakfast they slung their bags in the Jimny and took to the road again, this time enjoying the views as they went, and descending on Padstow harbour some forty minutes later. The picturesque town was surprisingly busy for the time of year, there was a party of camera-brandishing Japanese assaulting the quaint shops, and the large car park was swamped by foreign coaches. Richard hadn't expected this and was disappointed. After a hasty tour of both harbour and shops, they went on to Newquay but that was crowded too, and they couldn't decide where to stay for the night. Richard, trying to avert another quarrel, found himself suggesting that they return to the Haven. Despite its remote location, Richard had liked it there. For once, Kate agreed without further comment.

Two o'clock saw them pulling up outside the hotel. The freckle-faced Morwenna greeted them without a smile. "Didn't you like it 'down west' then?" Richard had told her of their plans to stay in Padstow for the rest of the weekend.

"There were too many tourists," he replied as beside him, Kate produced her plastic again. They booked the 'sea view' room for a second night; once settled they had a quick shower and then decided on a stroll.

The Haven's picturesque cove was busy this Saturday afternoon, but pleasantly so—not the locust stripping rush that Padstow had been. They ate a hearty late lunch in an adjacent café and spent the remaining afternoon beach combing; even Kate managed a smile as the late autumn sun appeared again and warmed her pale city cheeks.

Someone brushed passed Richard. He caught a scent: sultry, alluring, yet somehow stale—wrong. Curious, he turned but there was no one around. It was late afternoon now, light was fading fast and most of the day trippers had departed. They had the beach to themselves—well almost.

Movement caught Richards's eye. He turned to look toward that rocky place where the knife-edge cliff sliced hard into the ocean.

It was the redhead again—the one he'd seen last night. She stood there surveying the waves in silence, as she had before. Richard, captivated, watched as the wide hem of her shabby dress was soaked by a marauding wave. She failed to notice—so lost was she in her study of the waters. Richard felt rooted to the spot— there was something not right about this woman, and yet she fascinated him so. There was rawness... almost a hunger in the way she stared: she seemed lost to time and space, a stranger on a foreign shore. Should he go up to her? Perhaps she needed help. She lifted her head and Richard glimpsed pale features, comely in a strange, melancholy way. He took a step forward.

She turned, awarded him a withering glance. Richard froze: he felt odd, uncomfortable—pinned by that haggard stare. Different— she looked different, almost another person. He couldn't understand it, he was sure her hair had been auburn just now—he'd caught a brief sparkle of amber as the sun glinted off her curls. But the woman now staring so coldly back at him was no redhead; her hair was black and glossy as rain-washed coal. Strange—must have been a trick of the light, thought Richard.

And yet...? He felt exposed, awkward—it wasn't like him to gape so rudely at a stranger. Richard couldn't help himself—this was no happenstance meeting. He had a feeling he knew this woman—ridiculous notion though that was. She was a distance away but her expression was clear enough; loathing and revulsion—for him.

But why...? Richard shivered as a cold tingle crawled up his spine.

"Richard, what are looking at?" Kate's brittle bark broke the spell. He turned to see his wife staring at him in annoyed puzzlement. "You've been standing gawping at that big rock for five minutes. Whatever is the matter?"

"I... I thought I saw someone," Richard struggled, feeling foolish again. "It must have been the movement of light on the rocks over there. But she... they were so real, Kate."

Kate rolled her eyes. "You're going soft between the ears, Richard Harrison. Ever since you lost that job you've been away with the faeries. Are you listening to me?"

Richard hardly heard her; instead he tried to recapture that scent. Very subtle, a musky hint of violets—dangerous and alluring. Arousing yet somehow chilling too—disturbing. *Violets*—and how had he known that? Richard's botanical knowledge was basic at best, but there had been something oddly familiar about the scent. And he *had* seen her, damn it.

But where was she now?

"Fine." Kate had left him to his dreamy gawping and was already cutting a brutal path toward the hotel, but for once Richard wasn't that bothered. He stayed put awhile, striving to enjoy the peaceful gloaming and watching the waves shift in colour and hue—wondering (and daring to hope) if *she* would come back again.

But the woman was nowhere to be seen. She'd vanished like a wisp of salt spray, torn adrift by cutting breeze. Instead, a party of gawky teens armed with cans of Stella settled noisily close by and, squawking like rooks, began hurling rocks into the water amid shouts and hoots of laughter. Richard beat a swift retreat back to the hotel.

That night echoed the night before. Kate, aloof and frosty, retired early after dinner, leaving Richard with his drink wedged firmly between both palms. He should be feeling miserable, Richard told himself, after all, this weekend was all about bringing the two of them back together. But for some reason Richard hardly noticed Kate's going. Instead he gazed about the bar room listening to the jocular voices, soft Cornish brogues mixing with various other accents. The Haven Hotel was filling nicely: but then it was Saturday night. Richard, dreamy-eyed and relaxed, leaned back in his chair and soaked up the atmosphere.

He grinned when at ten past ten, a pony-tailed girl entered with a mandolin in tow, followed by two bearded guys in garish t-shirts armed with guitar and bass. Finally a sweating, greasy-haired drummer hauled his equipment into a corner and, after a natter and warm up with his fellow musicians, set upon it like a whirling dervish.

The band was great, their own particular Celtic twist on Hotel California had Richard strumming the table with his fingers and playing air-guitar. At some point some local lads offered him a game of pool and he, grinning broadly and armed with another whiskey, agreed.

It was gone two when Richard left the bar and stole into their musty room, to find Kate's neat sleeping face again lit by a watery moon. She'd left the curtains wide open and silvery light spilled into the room. Richard felt light headed—maybe it was the atmosphere, maybe it was the drink. He stared hard at his face in the mirror.

What's that...?

Richard's heart skipped a beat, and a cold shiver crept up his spine. For the briefest moment Richard thought that a stranger looked back at him from inside his own reflection.

My imagination—I'm drunk.

Richard relaxed and grinned stupidly: he was unshaven and

his hair dishevelled, but he was under the influence and didn't care.

Time to sleep. He snuggled up cosy beside Kate, letting the warmth of her soft body ease him into welcome sleep. Outside, the hunting moon was kidnapped by a fist of cloud.

* * *

She approaches in silence, her bare feet soaked and her torn hem washed with chilly brine. She looks up at the window of the inn: feels them sleeping there—the outsiders. Soon... the time for revenge had almost arrived. She turns triumphant to the shadowy silent figure beside her, and he smiles too. Both know that once this deed is done they will be free to roam again...

Chapter 4

The Lovers

NEARLY A MONTH PASSES AT Trewenny's Cross: December looms foggy and drear. Daniel receives a stiff letter from Father Padraig bidding him, in short blunt words, to be on with his penance and stop this idle prevarication—lest his weak soul be damned by hell-fire. Daniel is unmoved by the letter, defiant rather. He still has funds, though his coin is shrinking fast and he would have to find some work shortly: but not just yet—he still has time.

And he isn't worried about that; all his waking thoughts are on the girl, Sarah. They are hard lovers now, spending every free moment together. Now and then he'd feel a pang of guilt, and beat a purging track up the hill to the remote church hidden in its fold of ancient oaks. It was only two miles away—a beautiful setting, wedged deep in that wooded vale, descending almost down to the cliff top that reared so high above Haven Cove.

Once there, Daniel would talk to the Lord for a while and the Lord always understood him—even if Father Padraig didn't. Besides, the local Reverend Jolly was a kindly soul; he never questioned Daniel, and the Irishman in return saw no reason to divulge that he too was to be a man of the cloth, albeit an indifferent one—and Catholic too. Daniel suspected Jolly knew anyway, the Reverend had shrewd currant-eyes and besides, word perchance would have got out by now, though he'd mentioned little about himself and nothing outside of Trewenny's.

Daniel loved the sheltered churchyard with its quiet stones, he felt the peace of those that rested below and could think of no better place to end his days. He would always return from the church refreshed and full of zeal. Surely the Lord cared not but that his children were happy: all this bickering and strife made little sense. But Daniel was young, energetic and in love. He smiles as he strides briskly back down the hill. Rome and Father Padraig could wait for a wee while yet.

And Sarah Hosking was a woman to die for.

Her family had dwelt near Trewenny's since medieval times and were well respected, though of modest means. There were three sisters, all local beauties—though Sarah was the prettiest, in Daniel's opinion. He had met the family last Sunday and decided he liked Mr. Hosking well, and Mrs. Hosking (a fine looking woman herself) had warmed to him at once. Both parents seemed pleased that their youngest daughter was spending her time with such a well-mannered foreigner. Of course they knew nothing of Daniel's chequered past, and he wasn't about to divulge any of it. Sarah was taller than her sisters; her hair raven black, tumbling down her back in thick glossy curls. Her lips were cherry red and smiling, and her eyes...*those eyes*... they were the deepest, darkest blue, eyes that could set a man's heart on fire. And eyes a man would commit murder for.

For her part, Sarah loves Daniel. His dark quicksilver gaze excites her, and she is impressed by his sharp wit and cool confidence—so different to the local boys who were always dolefully predictable, whether kindly yet boring like poor Joe Collins, or moody and obstinate like the Cutting brothers.

* * *

Christmas comes and goes amid sleet and icy rain. Slowly winter yields its grip and eases into spring. Days lengthen and life takes hold again. Foxes prowl hungry in rain-sodden fields, and buzzards swoop lazily, questing for rabbits.

When the fields are yellow with the smiling faces of daffodils, Sarah leads Daniel to a place she knows well. A long walk over wind-combed grassy fields, down through tangled woods, with wren and thrush a-chatter, and robin serenading their way; and a lone roe deer shyly surveying their progress, before retreating wary into briar. Their destination is a sacred place (Sarah tells him), where the old folk came to be blessed by the kindly spirits that rumour said dwelt thereabouts. Daniel says nothing, but is intrigued.

Arm in arm they walk, on through the bird-noisy wood until they reach the joyful tumble of a silver, rock-strewn stream. This they follow until they reach a wide clear pool at the base of a high waterfall. Daniel smiles at the beauty of the place. The water of the pool is clean to look on and, (Daniel reaches down and brushes his fingers along the surface) cool to touch. A mirror: it reflects the reaching willow boughs that frame its perimeter, and everywhere the chiming chant of cascading torrent fills the spring air with metallic wonder. Daniel, glancing about, notices small rags tied to many of the branches surrounding the pool.

"What are those?" he asks Sarah.

For a reply, Sarah turns toward him and strokes his smiling face with pale playful fingers. "They're called 'jowds'," she tells him. "Many country folk believe there is an ancient spirit living here and, if appeased, she will heal the hurts of those who ask her. These jowds have been left by people who still follow the old ways—there's many such still living hereabouts."

"Pagans, you mean," Daniel frowns, he's not entirely sure about this place now. Certainly it is beautiful, but it was a bewitching, beguiling beauty, and it unnerved him slightly to imagine the strange practices that perchance have gone on here.

"Call them that if you want," continues Sarah, "but the villagers around here see no harm in preserving the old traditions. It's not that they aren't good Christians," she explains. "It is just that in Cornwall earth-magic is everywhere, and the early Celtic saints soon learned to tolerate these old ways—it's give and take, my love. The Celtic Christians were ever more tolerant than Saint Augustine's lot—you should know that." Daniel nods, but is uneasy.

"The customs still flourish to this day," says Sarah, "in secrecy. But as long as the congregation shows on Sunday, the churches hereabouts hold to contentment."

"It's the same in my own country, yes," responds Daniel. "And anyway those Celtic saints were Irish," he adds. "The only one that wasn't was Saint Patrick." Daniel laughs at the irony—it's lost on Sarah, but she smiles nonetheless. She likes the fact that he knows these things. Daniel leans forward, combs a wayward lock so he can better see her face. He laughs again. "Like me, most of them got lost on the way to Rome. I'm meant to be studying their journeys; well that's what I told Father Padraig in Galway. I'm supposed to be a priest, Sarah." Her eyes widen—though he's hinted at this before.

She smiles, after a moment's hesitation. She loves him—love finds a way through most walls men build, and Sarah is happy today.

I don't care...

"There is a well close by," Sarah tells him; "it was visited by St Piran long ago."

"I'd like to see that—so I would."

"We can go back that way. Now then, Danny—enough talking."

Sarah clasps Daniel's hand, and leads him through the withies to a sunlit glade, just a few yards away from the waterfall. There they disrobe and make eager love, unaware that they are watched by hateful scheming eyes.

* * *

Thomas squats uncomfortably and tries not to jiffle: his sweaty bulk is well hidden behind the scooped bowl of an ancient willow. He sees the lovers entwining in passion, his eyes drink in the white nakedness of Sarah's young agile body. He hears her moans and sighs: imagines himself on her, thrusting hard into her—even as the Irishman is now. He watches, hating ... lusting—captivated and compelled, soaking in every minute and 'feeling' her soft yielding cries as though they were meant for him.

He leans forward; Sarah is facing him now as she sits astride her lover. Thomas's eyes feast on her beauty, her black hair wild and free, her shoulders and arms, her small white breasts, those thighs—he glimpses the thatch of dark between. He shuffles his feet: a twig snaps. Thomas freezes.

"Who's there?" Daniel rolls free of Sarah's tight embrace. "Show yourself!" Daniel's eyes are wary and alert as they scan the creaking withies. "There's someone watching us," he whispers to Sarah.

"P'raps it's the old spirit giving us her blessing," giggles Sarah, but after seeing the serious look in Daniel's eye, she becomes scared. "Are you sure?" she asks him, now whispering too.

"I'll soon find out." Daniel leaps to his feet and, grabbing a large stick, approaches the thicket ahead.

Thomas, panicking now, scrambles backward and, turning noisily, makes a desperate dash into the dark undergrowth beyond with a furious Daniel giving chase, but the Irishman's naked body is trapped by tree limbs and briar, his soft skin lashed and torn—though in his fury he doesn't notice. Finally, and only after being pinned by hawthorn nails, Daniel curses and reluctantly lets the intruder get away.

"I'll be at you, so I will—yer sleekit shite!" Daniel shouts through the trees, but Thomas is well gone now. Sarah joins her lover after a moment, her eyes filled with worry.

"Who was it?" Sarah enquires.

"That lout from the inn—you know the big stupid-looking one with the gormless brother. I've had words with him before, so I have." Daniel's dark eyes are still scanning the bushes ahead. He is angry now, and decides upon paying a visit to those two brothers. "I reckon he's had a crush on you for a while now, Sarah."

Sarah, seeing the defiance in his gaze, clutches Daniel's arm. "He's called Thomas Cutting," she tells her lover. "I hate him." Her lips tighten as though she has swallowed something foul. "But be careful, Daniel, that one is black-hearted—the Treliggan Cuttings were always a strange lot, an' Thomas is the worst of 'em. Everyone knows that there is badness in him. You had better stay clear, my love."

"Well, we'll see about that." Daniel follows her back to the glade, where they both dress quickly in silence. Sarah is upset and Daniel's face grim, for him the magic of this place has gone now, gone forever. He vows to settle things with this Thomas Cutting in the inn at Trewenny's this very evening.

I'll stab the pair of them, so I will—and bugger me priestly vows.

They hurry back to the road passing St Piran's old well without a word, neither one now in a mood for stopping and making a wish. Sarah's pale pretty face is taut with worry, whilst Daniel's eyes burn like molten jet.

Chapter 5

The Mirror

RICHARD WOKE WITH A JOLT. He was cold—*so bloody cold*. And what was that sound? Something was tapping the window outside—scraping, drumming the glass. Richard turned his head slowly, not really wanting to look. A bird perhaps? Unlikely. It was still very dark, and way too early for birds. There it was again—a loud insistent rapping on the glass!

Tap scrape, tap scrape...

What the hell was it? And how could Kate sleep through such a racket? Fuzzy-headed and irritable, Richard lurched out of bed, cursing loudly as he stubbed a big toe on one of the nearby chair legs. Still grumbling he hopped and staggered across to the window for an angry peek.

Bloody thing...

There was nothing there. Nothing; just the wind bumping the shutters now and then. But no scraping—and definitely no bird.

Shit.

Richard rubbed his tired eyes and muttered as he looked out at the moonlit cove. The night sky had banished cloud, and the distant seawater spilled like mercury onto the even smudge of sand and pebble. All was serene and still—and yet somehow odd ... strange. Richard swore to himself quietly.

What's the matter with me? It's just the moon, for Christ's sake.

He was about to turn away from the window when something stopped him. Movement; shadowy out on the shoreline. Someone (or maybe something) was out there alone at this godforsaken hour. A fisherman perhaps, or shrimper maybe? Richard knew little about such matters but assumed it likely so. He leaned forward, tilted his head so he could see more clearly.

Richard froze.

It was *her*—that woman. Just standing and watching the ocean again. She was far away this time—right down at the water's edge. Somehow (he had no idea how) Richard knew she was calling out to him, warning him to be careful, and bidding him join her out there where wave brushed sand. Richard felt the tiny hairs rise on the nape of his neck, and bizarrely he felt his loins waken too. He stood gaping in the dark, frozen and naked at the window—his mind racing; fear, dread, fascination and desire, all were assaulting him now.

Who are you...?

As Richard's night vision cleared, he could see that her long dress was trailing in the dark-foamed water as the rhythmic breakers moaned and sucked about her feet. *She must be freezing out there*, thought Richard; perhaps she was unhinged—disturbed mentally. But there was power radiating from her skinny frame—some weird coercion, he couldn't stop gazing out at her. Just who was this woman, and what was she about? It didn't make any sense.

Several minutes passed; she didn't move—just stood there silent at her dreamy vigil. Still Richard watched from the window, he'd lost all sense of time and place, so compelled was he in his voyeurism. It was still chilly in the room, but he no longer noticed. Then he lost her, when a swift cloak of cloud cocooned the moon with sudden darkness.

Damn it!

She was gone, vanished with beach and surging waters. Total darkness had reclaimed Haven Cove, and the mystery woman's ragged silhouette had disappeared in the night. *Shit... and blast it...*

Richard shivered, feeling the chill again. He couldn't under-stand why it was so damn cold in the room now. The heater had made it stifling only a few hours earlier—and he hadn't tampered with the radiator (why would he?) he'd been drunk—but surely not that drunk? Richard left general maintenance and practicalities to Kate mostly—he was strictly 'white collar' and didn't like to get his hands dirty. Whereas Kate... well, she got things done, did Kate—just another chestnut for him to grind on.

Richard scratched an ear and shivered again. He was still standing bollock-naked by the window? Why? Suppose someone drove past and looked up? Richard smirked at that notion—not many joy-riders about tonight. Perhaps Kate was right. Maybe he *was* losing it and imagining things. Certainly he'd felt strange since coming here the other night.

The slippery pole—they'd be certifying him next.

I'm not crazy...

No, thought Richard: much more likely some evil little bas-tard had slipped something dodgy in his whiskey—those lads in the pub perhaps—just for the lark. Richard sighed, and cursed his throbbing head. He shivered; forced his gaze from the window, was about to return to bed when a soft noise stopped him in his tracks.

What was that?

Had someone spoken in his ear?

What the fuck is going on?

Richard could have sworn he'd heard a woman's voice whis-pering something urgently behind him.

He turned.

Nothing.

Get a grip, Harrison!

Then a woman's voice said... *Daniel...* in his right ear, and Richard's feet almost left the carpet. *Daniel...* he heard her husky voice again, this time over by the window.

Oh, God, please... what's happening to me?

Richard couldn't move for terror: he stood shivering and gap-ing like a hooked mackerel, as the creeping, icy dread gnawed into his nakedness. He slowed his breath and tried to summon calm—it was that last Bushmills for certain, some arsehole had spun him a Mickey.

But then who the bloody hell was Daniel?

That name was very familiar for some reason, it stirred a hidden memory. Richard pictured dark eyes mocking him, laughing at him. He felt a rush of sudden anger. *Get a grip, man!* Most likely some client who'd upset him back in the smoke—there had been many such back then.

I'm being stupid...

Richard eased a long slow breath into the room's chilly atmosphere. He watched it congeal and drift over to smear the window's damp glass. He turned away, took a step toward the bed.

And there it was again—the voice!

Daniel!

This time the woman's tone was clearer, and her hidden breath hissed through the room like vengeful steam. Paradoxically, Richard knew she was accosting him for some crime committed long ago. He felt culpable, guilty. But why? And just who the fuck was Daniel?

Richard's mind was racing, but his naked body was locked in terror trance. He remained close by the window—couldn't move—his wild eyes darting everywhere, his mind trying desperately to quell the rising sense of irrational terror swelling up inside his body. The room was bitter cold but Richard sweated now, despite the chill.

He felt certain something bad had happened here a long time past, and (ridiculously) that *something* had concerned him—but how could that be so? And why this stupid guilty feeling? He took another slow step toward the bed where Kate's blonde bob still showed above the sheets. Richard was shattered—needed to sleep.

He was hallucinating, was all—they'd drugged him, those local shitheads at the bar, (doubtless Ecstasy or uppers or some such thing—Richard, of course, knew little about such filthy stuff.) But he was very aware that things were fast getting out of hand.

Cold Turkey—like quitting fags, only worse. He recalled that motorbike film in the sixties—roll with it and let it wash over you, someone had said, or maybe that was another film. No matter, he would emulate that philosophy—a sharp injection of pragmatism was needed here.

But that wasn't working at the moment. Instead, Richard had the horrid certainty that he wasn't alone in the room with Kate. There was a third individual standing behind him. She (the whisperer) was standing somewhere over by the door. He could feel those hating eyes boring into his back, and was too terrified to turn, see who this was—though he suspected he knew that already.

It was *her*—the strange woman from the beach: it had to be *her*. But how stupid was that?—And why pick on him?

She had come for him—that was why. Returned from God knows where to punish *him* and him alone. But why?

Daniel...

Richard gasped, as a sharp stab of pain like a hot steely knife lanced deep into his stomach. He cried out, almost doubling over, but the lancing pain vanished almost as soon as it had come.

There was someone standing behind him now—he couldn't hear her, couldn't see her, but he knew she was there.

What do you want with me? Richard felt her icy breath coat the skin along his shoulder blades. He dare not look round. He counted to ten.

Eight, nine, ten... Richard could stand this no longer, torn between fear and weird fascination, he relented and turned toward the door behind him.

The door was open.

Wide open—it had been shut just a moment ago. Locked; by him when he returned from the bar. He'd pulled it to and turned the latch before clambering into bed. Richard clearly remembered doing just that, despite being tired and very drunk.

And yet now it was open—wide open.

Richard felt giddy, and his back ached from his rigid stance. Just how long had he stood here—moments... hours? He could not be sure. But still he couldn't move—not yet, and not while she was watching him.

What is happening to me? I want to sleep? I don't need this...

Richard warily scanned the vacant blackness beyond, still convinced someone watched him from the shadowy landing.

But no one stood out there. It was an empty space—the silent dark of hallway and stairs. Perhaps the latch hadn't closed when he'd shut the door—and yet he could have sworn he'd heard it click loudly as he'd pulled to. Perhaps it was a dodgy lock. No—Kate was funny about such things. The lock was sound—which was more than could be said for Richard's state of mind. He couldn't have shut it properly, despite feeling convinced that he had.

It must have been a draught, God knows, but it's cold enough in here.

Richard counted to ten a second time and then exhaled slowly, ordering his battered nerves to calm. This was all his imagination, he told himself, brought on by a cocktail of whisky and goodness knows what else—he'd have a word with that po-faced Morwenna in the morning, tell her about those lads and what they had done, maybe get them barred from the hotel—and serve the bastards right.

This morose behaviour just wouldn't do, however. He needed to get a grip fast. Kate was bound to wake in a minute: she'd have choice words—discovering him standing there, gaunt and starkers like a witless loon. Perish the thought—besides he'd had enough of this nonsense for one night. About time he took charge of himself.

Bolstered into motion by fear of Kate waking, Richard turned toward the bed again where his wife's face showed barely visible above the sheets.

He reached down to pull back the covers.

Daniel has come back for you...

The words were clear and cold—precise. Richard froze: he *felt* rather than saw movement out of the right corner of his eye.

Someone *was* watching him—here in the room. There was no room left for doubt. *She* was here.

Then Richard felt his gaze drawn inexorably to the mirror by the door. The long oval, shabby framed mirror—its glass gleaming with trapped moonlight. There was something else. Richard glimpsed a shadow flit across the reflected light. He looked closer; paled to chalk when he saw the face inside the mirror. Richard's jaw dropped, and a whimpering noise fled from his frozen trembling lips.

The face staring back at him was not his own.

It was the face of a young woman, her hair drenched and shiny from the sea, ragged and long—glossy black and curling. Richard could see weed and broken shells caught up in the tangled, dripping coils. Around her, the mirror's surface now seeped salty water, distorting her features; it dripped along the frame and ran down the wall in steamy beads.

The woman's eyes were unmistakable: he'd seen them before. They were filled with contempt and stalked him without mercy. Huge cold eyes—angry amethysts—icy and pitiless, they pinned him. Richard was a lamped rabbit—he could only stare and stare in the bitter chill. He couldn't move, he couldn't speak. He was bewitched—at the mercy of the woman in the mirror.

Her face was pale and drawn; beautiful, but lost—marred and distorted by the mirror's witchy sheen, like a face on a painting stowed for cobwebby years up in an abandoned attic. A masterpiece once, now long forgotten—discarded to dust and ruin.

She appeared way too thin, her features gaunt and lined—as though she were being eaten from within. Richard bit his lip—was dimly aware of the warm salty taste as the blood flavoured his mouth. Still, he couldn't move a muscle. Dread of her held him frozen in time.

And time was the key. But time held no power in this room—Richard realised that now. Outside a floorboard creaked in the landing, as though someone stood out there too. Perhaps another trapped soul seeking release from its prison.

Aside that—silence.

Even the hands on the clock had ceased to move, invisible fingers having muffled the dull click-clocking of Kate's bedside alarm. Richard was fading fast—he couldn't take much more of this.

Outside the moon waxed furious, its silver glow spilling eerie light into the room. Kate stirred, then lay still. Richard straightened slowly, cramp having taken his left leg unawares. He ignored the pain, kept his eyes locked on the face in the mirror. He felt like a fox caught fast in a snare—the wire tightening around his neck, as his heartbeat drummed inside his chest. As he watched, Richard saw the corner of her upper lip curl slightly—as though taking pleasure from his discomfort. Those amethysts were teasing him now, mocking and challenging him from deep inside the mirror—rapacious and hungry.

But for what and why?

Richard knew she was daring him to approach her, enter into her world. Almost he took a step forward, the cramp in his thigh having subsided. Then her lips parted slightly and her gaze misted over and, despite his fear, Richard felt his manhood stirring into sudden life. He blushed scarlet, feeling vulnerable and foolish—very aware, but the more he thought about that the harder it became.

Her eyes smiled at his blatant appreciation, and her lips parted a touch more. She was smiling openly now, beckoning him forward with a pale be-ringed hand—the fine blue veins showing clearly on her wet pale skin.

Richard was torn ragged between terror and desire. Forgotten was Kate, still sleeping only feet away from where he stood. Gone was the ache in his leg, so entrapped was he by the vision in the mirror. Richard was a prisoner tortured by the cruel promise of that capricious smile; an eager moth questing toward ecstatic oblivion. He no longer cared—all he wanted was... *her*. Somehow Richard knew he had only to step forward; reach out and caress that lovely ravaged face between his sweating, freezing fingers. Two, three steps—he would never know pain again.

He would never know anything again.

But that fear deterred him not. His raging lust was consuming him like fire: *I must have you...* Richard ached for her touch, could feel his sex burning down below. Desire had won. Banished now were fear, chill and numbing dread. *You are mine... mine!*

Richard felt his lips form a snarl: he was angry for her, savage—a hunter soon to sate his famine. She was the prey now, not him; he, Richard was the master—as should be.

Those eyes still dared him.

Come on... take me... Richard. Have me—you know you can if you enter inside the mirror's walls...

Richard raged inside; almost he felt another person had taken hold of him—a violent, bitter individual that wanted this woman nastily, way beyond normal comprehension. He'd lost control—gone was the confused banker, the embarrassed, self-doubting husband. Instead a brutal confidence washed through his veins. He moved at last; approached the mirror, stopping within easy reach of its misty glass. She watched him from within with wary eyes.

I am the strong one here... not you.

Richard felt his arms reach out toward her of their own volition, and he saw her smile widen further, noticed how her teeth were black and broken, and her breath fetid; it choked his nostrils with the damp rot of decaying meat.

But Richard didn't care about any of that. Nor did he see how her skin crawled slightly as though maggots were waking just below the surface. To Richard, she was beauty itself—that mocking smiling face in the mirror. She was his to possess and to own. His and no one else's.

She laughed then and the wheel turned one-eighty.

He was caught in her spell again—once more the victim. Trapped—happy fly waiting for the spider's deadly kiss. He didn't care—nothing mattered—just to touch her... feel her embrace. Richard reached for her face again, his cold hands hovering in front of the glass. Her eyes never blinked, but they narrowed to knifey flints at his approach, and she retreated back inside the mirror's depth. She was teasing him again—cruelly playing with his emotions.

Come inside... it's warm in this place...

Richard paused, his trembling hands scarce inches from the misting glass, and his feverish eyes now taking in the rest of her, as the mirror betrayed her secrets to him. Her blue-white skin glistened with damp moonlight. Richard could see that she too was naked beneath that soaking faded dress, and that her pale veiny limbs were wretchedly thin. The gossamer fabric clung to her small breasts, shrunken by the cold embrace of salty water. She was a creature of the ocean, and she had come to claim him. And he was willing—wanted nothing else. His fingers almost traced a line along the frosting glass.

You and I are one...

* * *

Morwenna woke when a heavy thud announced someone's presence in the landing outside.

Oh... so you're back...

She rolled over and closed her eyes again. She found it hard—did Morwenna—running this place alone since Dad had died, and Kev having left her for that slut down in Helston. She'd lost her mum years before. But Morwenna was a worker bee—she and her small staff of girls kept the Haven Hotel ship-shape. During summer she took on more staff—mainly to help out in the bar. Haven got swamped in the summer. Morwenna didn't much care for the tourists, but was more than happy to take their money. But this time of year the blow-ins were rare, so Morwenna had been surprised when the young couple had returned after their first night.

She didn't like the woman (Kate) very much—typical 'up-country' yuppie that one. But her husband seemed okay. Bit hen-pecked perhaps.

Another thud upstairs—louder this time.

Go away...

Morwenna's mind was racing tonight—not that she had much to worry her really, the hotel finances were in order and repairs all in hand. And she wasn't lonely—this life suited her taciturn nature. But still she was troubled by something—not the recurring noise in the night—that came and went. Morwenna had grown up with that. But something else troubled her as she lay silent in the dark. She got up after a few minutes dreaming, pulled the curtains back and glimpsed the moon riding a dragon of cloud into the west. The lane below was lit by its sheen. Nothing stirred. At last, satisfied with her perusal, Morwenna climbed back into bed.

But still she couldn't sleep. The thump came again, but she ignored it this time and shoved the pillow over her head.

Cold bloody murder... up there on the moor...

Morwenna opened her eyes. Had someone spoken—she wasn't sure. Then an image entered her mind; an odd occurrence long ago, back when she was a kid. An unpleasant memory; it hovered on the edge of her thoughts but she couldn't quite pin it down. Then she got it.

Morwenna sat up; she was wide awake now.

That was it—the man, Richard! She had seen him before—but where and when, Morwenna couldn't remember. It wasn't that his face was familiar either, but rather the way he acted; his manner, the shadow behind his watery gaze, and the way he faffed and fiddled at the bar—all things that reminded her of someone else.

Somebody Morwenna hadn't much liked.

But this was stupid; she'd never seen these guests before they arrived on Friday night. She was just overtired—worn thin. Morwenna sighed, *yes that's it—I'm overtired;* she blew a moth from her yellow lampshade and then resignedly slunk back inside the covers.

Morwenna shivered; it was cold in the room tonight, which was odd because the radiator was on max. Maybe the heating was cranky—she'd call Dave the plumber out, ask him take a look. Morwenna shrugged and yawned, closed her eyes and pictured the man called Richard's average face hovering in front of her. No, not Richard; another name and another place. Strange... it was a riddle, but Morwenna was sleepy now so she let it wash over her. She pulled the covers tighter to keep the chill at bay, and within minutes drifted off.

That following morning, the ever-pragmatic Morwenna had forgotten all about her strange feelings in the night. This, in light of what happened later that week, was somewhat surprising.

* * *

As sleep finally came for Morwenna, Richard Harrison still stood battling with his emotions in the room upstairs. Beneath the covers to his left, Kate stirred and moaned, but Richard didn't notice. Nor did he note the sudden banging of the shutters, as the early morning wind rode in on the rising tide. Spellbound and bewitched, Richard heard nothing but the soft sound of *her* breath. Kate, scarce two yards distant from where he stood, could well have been a thousand miles away—forgotten and deserted. Richard was oblivious to everything except the woman watching in the mirror. She was teasing him again now, beckoning him come forward, enter her domain. Still Richard hesitated, wrestling with himself—or rather with some other self that seemed to have taken part of him over—a darker, nastier Harrison that needed to dominate this woman who so cruelly mocked him.

Richard's greedy eyes drank in every inch of his tormentor. He saw the hard press of her nipples against the wet torn dress; he followed the curve of her fragile hips down. Saw what waited for him there, and could stand it no longer.

I need you!

Again, Richard's sweating hands hovered over the mirror's glass. Not a mirror, he realised now: a door—an entrance into another dimension and time. World within a world. A place where she and he could be lovers—as was meant to be. Richard had only to cross over and she would be his—forever. Simple. She nodded slowly, as though reading his thoughts. And perhaps she could.

Come in, Richard... my love, why do you delay? Do you love me no longer, dearest one?

She half turned away then, her eyes now angry at his indecision, gazing askance at him, and her soaked hair streaking like kelp across those gaunt cheeks and wanton mouth. Richard froze—felt his borrowed confidence slip again. This woman was playing him for a fool.

Then her mood shifted back again—changing hue like the ocean, her mistress. She was both mercurial and dangerous, this creature of his dreams. She saw his doubt, and anger fled swift as it had come. She smiled again now. Richard heard her whisper then.

Come, my love—there is little time left to us. Dawn is approaching fast!

She turned away again, now showing him her back. Richard felt the icy sweat slipping down his face. She was walking away from him! That frail body retreating and fading deep inside the mirror's depth! Richard felt a rush of sudden panic: she was leaving him! How dare she!

No, wait... I am coming! The scent of stale violets now filled the room, together with the rancid rot of old decay, and both those mingling with the briny steam, now rising up from her dripping hair as she walked away fading into the twilight of the mirror's heart. The cocktail of aromas filled Richard's foggy brain like heady wine. Enough.

You are MINE!

Then Richard's left hand touched the glass of the mirror and everything changed.

* * *

Laughter everywhere: all around him. Cruel and mocking—like steely barbs inside his head. The room screamed silent rage. The shutters flew open and the door slammed hard against its frame. A blasting chill tore inside the room, carried on a raging gust.

Deep inside the mirror, the woman's face had changed again. Gone were the smile and playful tease, and gone the lust in her eyes, replaced again by hatred and contempt. Her frail, bony hands now turned to scraping, reaping claws at her sides. She was back at the mirror's face now, her arms stretched out along its surface, and her long fingers scraping and clawing along the inside of the glass. Richard's head was spinning—he felt sick and giddy. The woman spat out at him, screaming the name *Daniel,* again and again and again—her bony fingers clawing for him, and her broken, bloody nails scraping dark red stains down the inside of the glass.

Richard recoiled as one struck by lightning. He felt numb, confused; his entire body now shuddered with violent convulsions. He was terrified now—more than before. He wanted to run, but still couldn't move. That poison gaze held him rooted to the spot.

Who are you...? Richard tried yelling at her, but his lips wouldn't move. He was paralysed and... *dying*—the bitch was killing him from inside that mirror.

Why—what have I done? Why do you hate me so?

For answer the woman's lips peeled back, and her eyes glared. There was nothing enticing about her now. Rather, she was skeletal and gaunt in her angry hunger. Richard was helpless, could only watch in growing terror as those moon-cast eyes worked their icy incantation on his already shredded nervous system. Web-caught fly: Richard waited for the spider's sinister approach.

And she came.

Fool—you are no match for me now...

* * *

Impossibly the mirror expanded, convexing outward—bulging like a wind-filled spinnaker sail, or else a huge silver bubble blown by some enormous child. It grew and grew, widening out, spreading along the entire wall; gone were door and bed where Kate still lay in silent, happy slumber.

Richard was forced back across the room, as the mirror swelled out toward him, becoming larger by the second; and her inside working the spell—still clawing at his face, trying to rake him bloody with those awful nails, or else poke his eyes out with jerky jabbing red-stained fingers.

But she couldn't reach him yet, not while she remained trapped inside the mirror-bubble. But still it expanded, swelling bulbous—a great dome—threatening to swallow the entire room, its outward motion pushing Richard back and back, until his shoulders slammed into the wall beside the window ledge. He gasped aloud—the only noise he'd managed—and held up a hand to ward off her attack. And from within she swiped out at him, screaming the name *Daniel* again and again, until that word rebounded off the walls. Richard's legs buckled; he slid to his knees, sweat-stained back sliding down the wall, staining the Laura Ashley wallpaper behind: he covered his ears.

No more. He could take no more. Richard could feel his heart pounding, reaching bursting point in his chest. *I am dying...*

He made a noise—a pathetic moan, again, the only sound

he could manage. The damp cold texture of the mirror was hard against his face now, smothering him. Richard tried to shuffle sideways, but to no avail; the mirror filled out either side of his trapped body and ran along the wall behind him. *Help me... someone...* Richard was pinned helpless. He closed his eyes, felt his consciousness slipping away. He was falling into darkness.

But that brought no escape: the woman was waiting for him inside his head, as Richard tumbled he heard her shrill, hating voice screaming in his ears. Then his head slammed against the floor. He puked—opened his eyes. She was crouched low over him, her rancid breath choking his nostrils.

Please...

Her eyes were owl-large, dark like raging storm cloud. They glared triumphant, only inches from his face. Richard passed out again at that point. But she wasn't finished with him yet. She clawed at the glass; scrape and slide, scrape and hammer.

Then finally her nails broke through the glass, and scored a savage line down the side of Richard's left cheek. He woke screaming—finding his full voice at last. Richard was a mess: his mouth smeared greasy with vomit, and his cheek burning and oozing blood. Adding to that, he was now choking with the weight of the glass pressed against him.

Then the bubble burst open, sending icy shards of mirror like so many lethal knives thudding hard into the walls. The sound was like a bomb exploding next to him, his ears rang and his head pounded. Richard covered his face with his arms and wept; he hunched low and shut his eyes, but was mercilessly slashed to ribbons by the mirror's flying shards. Richard yelled and yelled, as bright blood coursed down his arms, pouring over his knees to pool in dripping puddles at his feet. At last the slivers ceased. Richard's shouts subsided to a dismal sob.

No more—please...

Richard could feel his mind caving in, slipping down deep into the pitiless void where she would be waiting for him again. He lost consciousness again, falling—down and down deep into the black.

* * *

"Richard!"

Kate's voice... calling me...

"Richard!" Light filled the space behind his eyes. The nightmare was over—or was it?

I am alive...

Richard Harrison opened his right eye slowly, half expecting it to fill with blood. But instead the salt of a single tear traced down his cheek and watered his mouth.

"Richard—what's wrong with you?"

Kate was sitting bolt upright in the bed, her face far from compassionate. "For Christ's sake talk to me, will you! Why are you lying on the floor? Have you been sick?" Kate's expression shifted from irritation and confusion into outright annoyance and disgust. "You look like you've seen a bloody ghost!" Kate said. "Are you ill? Talk to me!"

Richard didn't respond. He wiped his mouth and blinked at the mess he'd made on the carpet. He didn't care—it had been a dream.

Thank you, God!

Kate watched him in silence as Richard—almost cheerfully—surveyed the room; no blood, no broken glass, and no *her*.

Thank God. Over by the locked door, the mirror hung lifeless. Richard felt a wash of relief flood through him. His knees ached and his head throbbed and he felt like shit. But hey, he was alive. It had all been just a stupid dream. The workings of his drug-induced imagination brought on by some shit-arsehole lacing his whisky. The relief was wonderful. Richard grinned across at Kate; the gormless gape did little to soften her demeanour. "I... I just had a bad dream," Richard said weakly.

"I'm sick of you, Richard Harrison," Kate said, as he climbed back into bed, shaking and shivering. "You're bloody freezing." She rolled, showed him her back, "and you had better wash that carpet too—else Morwenna bills us." Richard didn't respond; instead he stared up at the ceiling and counted his blessings.

* * *

Half hour later, Kate was out on her run. Richard stayed in bed, surfacing only as she returned red-faced and panting into the car park outside. While Kate finished off with some stretching by the wall, Richard made haste to dress, make the bed and act as if he had a plan. He felt like grinning—he'd survived whatever those gits had done to him last night. He'd been sure he was going to die at one point.

Time for payback.

When Richard plumped the pillow, something small and purple fell into his lap. He reached down, carefully grasping the object and then, recognising what it was, Richard felt suddenly sick again, his already pasty skin bleaching white as classroom chalk.

It was a faded violet—tiny, crushed and wan.

Kate found him sitting there on the bed, his features morose. She rolled her eyes, fumbled deep into her bag for her iPhone; within minutes Kate was gone again. Moments later, Richard heard the Suzuki roar out of the car park and scream like a banshee up the lane. He closed his eyes—must have slept for a time.

Chapter 6

The Fighter

LATER THAT AFTERNOON, DANIEL SITS brooding in the corner of the inn at Trewenny's Cross. He takes a long pull on his tankard; watches the grey winter rain sheeting down upon the muddy track outside, already forming large brown puddles, and doing little to improve his mood. Sarah was away to her duties cleaning in the rooms upstairs and he, Daniel, had been in no mood for words after their encounter with Thomas Cutting at the waterfall earlier today. He takes another pull at his jug and glares hard at the rain—his rare mood worsening by the minute.

I shall sort you proper, Thomas Cutting... you wait and see— God blast me, but so I shall.

Dusk finds Daniel still at his cups; he watches quietly as slowly the inn fills, as evening beckons and the grey day falls to dusky gloom. Inside, the atmosphere grows thick with tobacco and log smoke. Daniel drinks and waits.

It is quite late when the Cutting brothers lumber into the inn, slamming the door shut behind them with customary subtlety. Thomas glances briefly at Daniel seated over in the corner; he smirks, and then turning away, mutters something funny in his brother's ear. Robert shows his toothless smile and mutters back, his thick tones just as incomprehensible as his brother's. They receive their frothing ale-jugs from Big John, and shuffle noisily across to the far side of the room. Here, they claim two vacant stools and seat themselves down amid scowls—wrapped in their thick coats, the brothers resemble nothing more than two shabby sacks beneath the candlelight.

Daniel, just sober enough to realise he'd drunk far more than was planned for this evening, watches them smirk and whisper.

Ugly bastards...

To hell with it! Daniel Flannigan is well fired up now and bristling for a fight. At last he can take it no longer; Daniel pushes the table back, stands for a moment slightly shaky, and then makes brisk and angry for the far corner. The Cutting brothers watch him approach in wary silence. Thomas's bloodshot eyes are full of challenge. Just then Sarah emerges from upstairs, her bare white arms laden with blankets. She freezes, seeing her lover calmly walk across to the table behind which the Cuttings squat idle on stools. Daniel's eyes are flinty chips of hate. Sarah exchanges worried glances with Big John, who shakes his head and tugs his beard.

"I've some words for you outside, if you're man enough to hear them." Daniel's soft Irish brogue cuts through the thick atmosphere like a cleaver hewing steak. Hushed voices stop mid-sentence, and dingy faces stare across to where Daniel now stands fiery-eyed, glaring down at the slouching, sulky bulk that is Master Thomas Cutting.

Thomas turns to his brother and grins. He slurps noisily at his ale jug, grins again, and then hurls both content and vessel hard at Daniel's face.

"Fuck your words, Irishman—you've too many of those as it is!" Thomas leaps to his feet, swinging free with the heavy cudgel he'd kept hidden beneath his trench coat.

Daniel ducks from the tankard's sailing path; he glimpses it clatter loudly into a nearby vacant chair, spraying an old feller with frothy brew. He catches Thomas's cudgel mid-swing and yanks it towards him, tugging the bigger man off balance. Thomas cusses and grunts; he tries to free his weapon but Daniel, stepping closer, rams his left elbow hard up under the bigger man's fat chin, and

Thomas's head snaps back with a jolt.

Now Robert Cutting is on his feet, yelling and rushing to assist his struggling brother. Daniel, quicker by far than the sluggish Robert, releases the stave and leaps behind the adjacent table. He kicks it forward hard and fast into Robert's midriff, causing the younger Cutting to buckle forward in winded pain.

"Useless bastards, the pair of ye!" Daniel squares on Thomas, who is now bulling up for another swing. The cudgel whooshes over Daniel's head as he dives low, and using that head as a missile, makes brutal contact with Thomas Cutting's ruddy face. Crack! The bone crunches on impact—leaving Thomas's nose now bent and broken. His upper lip is split also—Daniel laughs—looks a right mess now, does big-lad Thomas.

Thomas isn't finished yet; coughing blood and spitting, he launches his weapon's knobbly head hard at Daniel's face. Daniel jumps back, again anticipating the move; he knocks the heavy stick aside, again sending Thomas's blow wide.

"My sisters make better scrappers than you, big shite!" Daniel kicks hard and sharp into Thomas's groin. Thomas grunts, slumps to his knees, and throws up enthusiastically on the rushed slate flags.

Daniel chuckles, as the bigger man coughs and dribbles out a cocktail of beer and blood and spew. He contemplates giving Thomas another kick to finish him good, but a blow from behind sends him reeling. Daniel's head spins, he loses his balance.

Fucking craven shite hit me from behind...

Daniel tries to stand up straight, but his vision is blurred and he is seeing stars. Over on the stairs, Sarah is tugging at John's sleeve and yelling in his ear. Big John, having seen enough, decides to put an end to this.

Robert, cudgel in hand and spitting obscenities, steps in to strike again. His swing is checked though, and he loses his chance, when two massive arms grip him from behind and hoist him backwards, nearly lifting his feet off the floor.

Big John Nicholls the innkeeper hurls Robert Cutting across the room; the boy crumples when his head impacts on the oak lintel above the fire. Daniel, partially recovered from his giddiness, decides he hasn't finished yet. He wades in on the still-retching Thomas, ignoring his own cracked skull and spinning head. Spitting and cussing, Daniel aims another kick at Thomas, but John stops him, pulling him back by his collar and cuffing him twice across the head.

"Enough! Yer silly bugger," Big John says. "I'll not have scrapping in here, you can piss off outside in the rain and tear each other's ears off—and to hell with the pair of you. Not you—yer daft twat!" This last to Robert Cutting who, though nursing a bleeding head, had once again retrieved the heavy stick and was again preparing another vengeful swing.

"Give me that stick, boy." Big John holds out his hand, and reluctantly Robert Cutting wanders across and hands over the weapon. He then slumps back onto a stool in sulky defeat. "You're soft in the head, young Robert," John tells him. "Big brother set you up to this, didn't he?" Robert nods wearily. "I dare say you'd jump off Pendarrow Point if Thomas told you to," John tells him. "Go home, boy, and don't hurry back—else I'll do the ear-clipping next time." Robert nods wearily and then, defeated, shuffles out the door.

But Sarah gets to the doorway quicker; she spits in Robert's ear just before he vanishes outside. "You heard what John said, Cutting—don't come back!" Sarah yells, as he shuffles silent out into the rain.

* * *

Meanwhile, Thomas and Daniel stand glaring at each other in frosty silence. Thomas's mouth has already swollen badly, and his battered nose still drips blood. He wipes his smeared face with a grubby sleeve, smoulders at Daniel for a moment longer, and then shoulders past him, making for the door leading out to the courtyard beyond.

Daniel follows: "Heh, yer big shite—I've not finished yet!" Sarah tries to stop him, but Daniel pushes past her and makes for the door, ignoring Big John's warning from behind.

But the brothers were no longer in the mood for fighting. By the time Daniel reaches the courtyard with John fast behind him, the brothers have already left. Sarah, joining them, points and laughs, seeing the two soggy figures squelch down the lane, before disappearing in the murky dark beyond. Again Daniel makes to follow, but John rests a meaty palm on his shoulder.

"Leave it, lad," he says. "It's time you cooled down a jot." Sarah, having only just cooled down herself, now looks worried. Despite that, her moist eyes are filled with love and pride as she gazes up at Daniel. For his part, Daniel winks at her and grins defiance.

"Irishman," says John, interrupting the two, "Do not take offence, but I think you better leave here tomorrow." Daniel raises a quizzical brow. "I suggest you venture up Devonshire way," continues John, "there's more work up there, boy—or so they tell me," he says.

"It's not that I don't like you, lad," John adds. "I do. But they two buggers will be back for more presently. You, lad, won't be safe here in Trewenny's after dark."

"I'll not be parted from Sarah," replies Daniel. "I didn't start this, John; you know it was those bastards—so it was."

John is unmoved. "I've watched you stewing all evening, laddie," he says. "No. You've brought this on yourself, Master Daniel—I'm sorry to say it." John wipes the sweat from his brow and scratches his ear. "You're banned from the Cross, my lad—it's for the best. You can sleep here tonight for free—but I want you gone at first light."

"Then I'm going with him," states Sarah, placing herself firmly between Daniel and her employer. "I love Daniel, John. I mean to stay with him always."

"You belong here, Sarah Hosking," responds John scratching his ear again. "I promised your father, William—may God rest his honest soul—that I'd see you come to no harm, girl. This lad's decent enough, but he's a scrapper, and I'll warrant a ladies' man too. He's a roving eye, has young Danny boy, most likes he'll have found another wench to warm his bed in a week or two."

Daniel shakes his head to this last comment. "No chance of that," he says glaring hard at John.

Big John ignores him, his kind eyes still on Sarah. "You're young yet, girl," John continues, "and better off forgetting this wild laddie."

But Sarah knows her own heart, and is not dissuaded. And so that very next morning she abandons her post at the Inn at Trewenny's, despite Big John's protestations and Elizabeth's worried frowns. Hand in hand, Sarah and her lover make for the nearby coast. Here her aunt (a recent widow) lives quietly in a small cottage, on the edge of a pretty wave-washed hamlet called Haven—named after the rocky cove surrounding it.

Chapter 7

The City

RICHARD HAD HARDLY ACKNOWLEDGED KATE'S return from her recent trip. He didn't think to enquire where she'd gone—even though that was over two hours ago. He just sat there on the crumpled bed, moping in silence and still gazing down at the faded flower in his palm. What was happening to him? That business last night he'd thought a dream—but now...?

Richard felt a weird connection to that woman—but how and why? It didn't make any sense. Richard was worried this morning—very worried. Perhaps he *was* losing it? But then—where had these violets come from?

A thought crossed his mind like a sudden ray of summer sun. *Unless these dried flowers are part of the wind-up too.*

Maybe Morwenna was in with those arseholes who'd laced his Bush. Richard now suspected conspiracy—a Machiavellian collusion, rife throughout the entire Haven Hotel. Torture the tourists—Richard had heard about this sort of thing. Well, he'd caught them at their game. Good job too. Richard would have to alert the manager (whoever he was) about their behaviour at some discreet moment, (no need for Kate to know.)

He felt better now—more sorted, in control for a change. But one thing still troubled him—the woman on the beach. He'd fancied her—that was all. Simple enough, really.

And then that drug-induced dream had turned her into a fiend of his own creating. It was all pretty Freudian stuff—he supposed.

Despite his new hope, Richard couldn't free his mind from the phantom woman who had visited his dream last night. She had seemed so real. Again, he pictured her naked in the mirror, and felt a sudden pang of guilt at the renewed stirring in his loins. But it wasn't right—fancying a ghost. Richard shuddered, remembering what had followed in that dream.

Enough! Richard barred that image from his mind, focussing instead on the fading Laura Ashley wallpaper, and stubbornly counting to ten. Then he remembered the stain he'd made on the carpet, and lurched yawning for the bathroom; here, Richard rinsed a facecloth with cold water, and then half-heartedly wiped at his deposit. Cleaning up—Kate's province, normally. After his indifferent efforts, Richard rinsed the cloth clean in the bath, yawned again, and then retired to stretch out on the duvet. It was all too much. Richard, (only thirty three), now suspected he was embarking on a fully frontal mid-life crisis.

Kate had again departed without acknowledging his surface from stupor. She'd vacated the room in icy silence before he could say, "How's your morning been, darling?" Half hour passed, Kate returned red-faced from those hectic business calls to her virtual office. Kate was always calling someone back there. One of her coven no doubt, sharing commiserations on what an arsehole she had married.

Entering their room for the third time that day, Kate finally awarded her husband a withering stare.

"You look like crap, Richard," Kate told him before ramming her iPhone into its charger and switching on. It buzzed and winked at her, but Kate ignored it. "How much did you drink last night?" Kate asked him frostily.

"Not a lot," Richard mumbled, bleary-eyed. "But someone slipped something in my whiskey, Kate."

"Oh sure." Kate wasn't listening—but then she never did. She washed her hands in the en-suite sink and dried them off with customary fastidiousness; she then rinsed her mouth out with that dreadful purple stuff she used to make her breath enchanting—all the time ignoring Richard. Then she spied the facecloth lying damp and crumpled in the bath. Kate viewed it suspiciously; she picked it up and sniffed at the contents. *Ugh!* Kate pulled a face and gingerly washed the cloth anew—kneading soap into the flannel and then rinsing out again with cold clear water. Richard watched her every move.

Fussy bitch.

"No shit, Kate," Richard said then. He looked indignant as he watched his wife deftly wring the facecloth dry, and then return it to its correct position on the towel rail. Richard feigned indifference, he was starting to feel pissed off now and hard done by. He'd had a rough night, and what did she care? *Bitch-cow.* "I've felt sick all night, and had nightmares you wouldn't believe whenever I finally managed to drift off."

Kate raised an eyebrow. "Serves you right for getting pissed again," she said. Kate shed her denims on the floor and clambered into a freshly ironed pair. She changed her shirt too—though the abandoned one had been fresh on this morning after her run, and was spotless.

"Kate—I'm not joking, they rigged me a Mickey Finn. I don't usually hallucinate on whiskey." Kate shook her head and fumbled for her purse.

Bitch—you never believe anything I say these days.

"I'm driving to Truro this afternoon," Kate announced, having checked the purse's content, "for late lunch and shopping. What you do is entirely up to you."

"Oh, I'll tag along," Richard responded defeated again; he now felt like an unwanted puppy.

"Kate's nod was indifferent. "We'll leave after coffee." Simple as that.

* * *

An hour later (having missed out on breakfast and brunch), Richard yawned in the passenger seat while Kate launched the

Jimny down the A30. The local radio blasted out the latest number one. Richard winced, and pressed the search button.

They crested a rise; Richard watched a field of wind turbines—each one turning in perfect timing to Floyd's 'Brick in the Wall'.

He dozed, vaguely aware of Kate cutting someone up on a roundabout. Richard left her to it and shut his eyes. He found himself yet again dwelling on the rigours and peculiarities of the previous night. Richard now doubted his earlier conspiracy notion as too glib—just himself covering up what really had happened. And something *had* happened—of that much, Richard felt certain.

But what to make of it?

Either some spiteful shit was playing with his dick in the dark, or (much scarier), Richard was hearing voices and seeing visions, weirdly erotic and terrible visions. And those shards had cut him—oh, he had felt that! No dream could be *that* real—surely? Besides, even a loaded whiskey wouldn't have affected him that badly, and he had been sober when he saw *her* on the beach, both times—well relatively sober anyway.

But there'd been two women in that dream last night. One, the mysterious beauty from the beach; the other—the one she had changed into, her alter-ego—a witch, or a changeling perhaps? Richard knew nothing about this stuff. But both women had one big thing in common—they hated Richard.

Join the club...

Richard, now feeling carsick, closed his eyes and shuddered.

I won't let this get the better of me.

Determined, Richard finally ceased his morbid reverie and, mind now resolute, focussed instead on the road ahead.

Kate anchored up in a car park near the cathedral; she retrieved a ticket out of the machine and then thumbed it onto the windscreen. The ticket said 15.00. That gave them two hours—hardly enough time to enjoy the delights of the city. When Richard suggested longer, Kate glared at him and responded that the pubs were already open, so why was he complaining. Then, without further word or hesitation she left him gaping, and cut a ruthless path down toward the first clothing store, on a rapacious quest for bargains. Richard left her to it, happily.

I hope you choke on your charge card.

He was content just roaming the busy streets for a time, trying in vain to sort his head out. He'd make for a coffee house, he decided. A mug of strong, black filtered Italian would soon steer some sense back into him—that, and a prawn-mayonnaise baguette. Richard trudged on, shouldering his way through a party of teenage girls; they ignored him (and each other) as they deftly texted gossip from their multi-coloured Smartphones.

Passing close to the cathedral entrance, Richard decided to take a look inside. He'd never been overly religious, but last night had scared him badly. He was still hung up about that bloody woman and how her face had changed into such a horror. Perhaps she'd bewitched him, and now Richard needed exorcising or something?

But who to ask—and how? There were bound to be protocols. But that no longer seemed appropriate, now he was inside these hallowed walls.

It's just my mind working against me. There had to be an explanation. Maybe it was just that the room was haunted back there, and the randy ghost had taken a fancy to him. Why not—I mean stuck in an attic for three hundred years—got to be boring, hasn't it? Richard smiled at the concept of a horny ghost. But why not? Stuck out there in limbo for generations—must be lonely, that, even for a ghost. Richard suspected weird shit like that happened sometimes—he'd watched enough stuff on Sky. Life was an iceberg—we only see the top bit, but it's that big cold bugger under the water that takes us out. Richard pictured Kate Winslet with her arms out wide and winced, recalling how his own Kate loved that movie.

But. And it was a big 'but': If that room was haunted, then why hadn't Kate noticed anything? No, Richard knew this was to do with him; either he was deluded (bad enough), or (far worse), he was being stalked by a horny ghost with a murderous doppelganger who made Mack the Knife look like Mary Poppins. Absurd and paradoxical though all this was, Richard knew he was, or rather *had* been involved with that woman in some way. But when... and where? And how ridiculous a concept? And anyway, how could such a thing occur?

Richard decided to linger awhile inside the cathedral. He felt daunted by the vast gothic arches and the serene quiet emanating from within, but despite that, took comfort just from being here. He was worried though—he'd been thinking stuff that no one should be thinking inside a cathedral. Rude stuff—bad stuff.

What if God was listening?

Chastised into sobriety, Richard humbly made for the back row of vacant pews. There, he sat quietly for a moment's intense contemplation. Meanwhile behind him a squadron of camera-wielding geriatrics mustered eagerly; they swarmed, hovered, and soon began talking (much too loudly in Richard's opinion), about the construction and beauty of the building they were in. Why did people always have to talk? Why couldn't they just shut up and soak in the atmosphere? Surface feeders the lot of them, thought Richard.

Go away...

Aside the aging avids, there were only one or two people milling about, so Richard was left to his thoughts. And sitting there in contemplative silence, Richard felt an inner calm slowly asserting itself. He was on the turn—bolstered by sudden piety and all things decent.

Richard Harrison would face this thing (whatever it was) head on, and seek out some brisk answers. His head was clearer now that he'd decided on a positive course of action. He would have that coffee and baguette, and then seek out a museum; the library, or else an old bookshop—anywhere that would have information on ghostly activity and hauntings in North Cornwall. Richard needed to clarify if he were imagining things, or this really was some dark secret known only to those who regularly frequented the Haven Hotel. Neither option was overly pleasant, but Richard had to know—one way or another.

Bolstered and determined, Richard vacated Truro Cathedral, now cutting a brisk path through the busy streets, trying to steer clear of the deep gutters that runneled along the curbs—ankle-breaking booby traps, each and every one.

After two large strong coffees, a sweaty baguette, and another focussed walk, Richard (feeling decidedly better) discovered a second hand bookshop, down a side alley on the outskirts of the city centre.

Once inside the cluttered (but immaculate shop), Richard asked the polite (but slightly puzzled) bespectacled gentleman behind the desk about ghosts and such like. The man pointed over to a gloomy corner of the shop. A stapled sign announced: 'Otherworldly Section.' Here, battered paperbacks were stacked precariously high in semi-ordered heaps.

Richard spent at least an hour in that dusty corner. He'd told the shopkeeper he was looking for something specific; the polite chap had just shrugged and left him to it, doubtless hopeful that he would eventually purchase something. Occasionally other customers entered, and brief courteous words were exchanged. Richard, busy in his corner, was ignored on every occasion, just as he was equally oblivious to their comments on the weather and state of 'old so and so's lane' this winter.

Richard industriously thumbed over copious dusty copies of spooky tales and creepy yarns. He learned about giants and witches; some place called the Gump, Willo the Wisp; not to mention Knockers and Spriggins and Piskeys—a veritable Cornish cornucopia of otherworldly critters. Richard (not usually a fan of such fairy stuff) was quite captivated by it all. He trawled through shabby tomes shedding faint illuminations on this or that grisly murder; those poor souls up in Bodmin Gaol, and there were hints concerning certain capers performed in some dreary wood near Padstow. It was all riveting stuff.

But none of it relevant—and he could hardly spend all day in here—much as he'd like to. But it was already 2:30 pm and Richard's time was running out. Just when he was about to quit from his exhaustive perusal, Richard found what he'd been seeking (and dreading.)

A book titled: *'Queer Tales from North Cornwall'*.

Inside the battered covers, Richard found a stained paragraph about Trewenny's Cross, concerning some dire event on the beach near Haven Cove, well over a century ago. Richard felt an icy shiver trace the length of his spine. A girl's name—he couldn't quite make it out, the text was faint and faded. And there a mention of the same girl and her lover, but it was almost illegible. Richard didn't hesitate; he stood cursing as the cramp took his thigh again, and then shoved the shabby book on the counter for the man to price.

"I can't say I recall seeing that one before," the owner of the shop said, as he neatly stuffed Richard's important purchase in a paper bag. Richard just grinned at him, and squeezed out through the doorway. Despite being only fifty pence the richer, the book-seller looked decidedly relieved at his departure.

* * *

As Kate drove out of the city, Richard fumbled in his paper bag and scanned his purchase. With goose bumps and dry mouth he read on: it was difficult to decipher, the ink had faded so badly and the text was antiquated. Despite that, Richard gritted his teeth and read on in tight-lipped fascination.

The relevant paragraph was headed: *The Haunting at Haven Cove.*

Richard shivered, and shut the book. He would wait until they got back—didn't have the courage at the moment.

* * *

That evening after dinner, again Kate left him to it. She was still angry with him, but at least she seemed resigned to letting him continue as he wished. At reception, Richard demanded to see Morwenna, but it was her night off, Angela, the other girl, said.

"She's doing her Pilates class today," Angela announced, as though that were relevant. Richard had shrugged, nonplussed. He had no idea what Pilates was—sounded like some old Greek guy.

"Well, I'll see her in the morning," he'd said, and made briskly for the bar again. After another pint, he found his courage and opened the scary book. Thumbing through tentatively, Richard reached the passage on Haven Cove. As Richard read the faded words, his face paled and the atmosphere in the bar chilled around him.

Cold blooded murder—up there on the moor...

* * *

She wanders back through the time gate—sees herself at that earlier time, a young girl happy and full of hope. He is with her, too—though he is not as he once was. He is cruel now—unforgiving, as is she. They have paid a high price—choosing not to cross but rather to await their chance.

Neither has any room for remorse—these two have waited long for this fruition. Many souls have passed since their mortal parting; bodies lost at sea, drowned mostly, though some pulled in under the waves. The two of them have searched and searched but still *he* evaded them.

But fate's wheel had turned fully upon itself; at last they had found the one they sought. She had almost broken him last night. This time she would finish it—she and her lover would be free at last!

Chapter 8

Hobbling Tom

THOSE WERE HAPPY WEEKS SPENT down at Haven Cove; Susan Harvey is a kindly soul, and her little cottage just big enough for Sarah and her beau to lodge in. Susan, though disapproving at first, knows well what it's like to love, and then lose that love—so she turns a blind eye to the youngsters and, enjoying the conspiracy, keeps Daniel's presence at her cottage a secret. Sarah often sees her family these days—she tells her mother Daniel has gone away, and that she is helping dear Aunt Sue down at the cove, now that Big John has kicked her out of Trewenny's.

For his part Daniel stays handy, chopping wood and clearing drift and flotsam from the sea-washed track. He helps Susan with many of her chores—hers is a hard dreary existence down here alone, it's been over a year since her fisher husband, Ben, was lost out at sea. She never complains though, and Daniel admires her for that.

Aunt Susan likes Daniel too—she believes this urgent business between her pretty niece and the charming Irishman will burn out at some point. Daniel was a rover—that much was apparent, and dear Sarah would settle down with some nice local boy in due course. But let them enjoy this time they have—however brief. For the moment, Susan likes having them around. She basks in their joy, remembering fondly that distant time when she, Susan, had the prettiest face in the parish.

Come summer, Daniel finds labour on a farm near Port Isaac, some miles further down the coast. It is far enough away from Trewenny's Cross to avoid recognition, but near enough to able to travel by pony to and fro. Too exhausted by his labours to make that journey every day, Daniel takes cheap lodging at the farmstead. Most nights he visits the tavern down on the quay, but on Saturdays Daniel rides back east and joins Sarah at the cottage at Haven Cove.

Sarah misses Daniel while he is away, but knows this is for the best—besides, the coin he returns with each week helps all three of them. And so for a while, things work out well and all parties are content.

But life never stays the same, even at Haven Cove, and happiness is but a fleeting chance awarded to some lucky few for a brief while. There is always someone ready to pour cold water on other people's joy. That someone on this occasion is a crippled old gossip—called by most folk, Hobbling Tom.

* * *

They'd told him the Irishman had left—Big John and the others. He'd heard that Sarah was down at Haven Cove staying with her aunt. Thomas had been down there twice during summer—on both times he'd seen Sarah and her aunt too. The pair seemed inseparable. Thomas still stews over the thrashing he and Robert got from that foreigner. Word had spread like wildfire throughout the parish about how he and his brother had been made to look like fools—Thomas dare not show his face in the 'Cross these days.

He keeps a tight lip, and stays busy with the farm all summer. He'd leave Sarah be for the moment: sooner or later she'd be back at Trewenny's. Thomas would seek her out then. He'd apologise for his behaviour, say he'd only been looking out for her safety—worried that that Irish fellow meant her harm—what with his glib tongue and over easy manner. Sarah would see sense and in time he, Thomas, would win her round. There were few eligible bachelors left in Trewenny's these days, discounting soppy old Collins and several other lack-wits. Sarah could do much worse than take Thomas Cutting for her husband. So Thomas eventually convinces himself, throughout that long hot summer. He has only to wait, and Sarah will be his. She could do a lot worse, Thomas thinks again.

* * *

Daniel makes a few friends down there on the quay. During those long summer evenings, he helps mend nets and joins in crabbing and such social activities. They spend a deal of time in the inn too—he and his work fellows, when freed from their duties back at the farm. The farm is only a mile from the busy port, and with not much going on back there, Daniel seeks out what company he can find in the inn by the quay. He plays cards with some of the fishermen and the occasional trader. Daniel is good at cards and usually wins. He is popular and most people enjoy his company, even when he beats them at cards.

Warmth with summer eventually passes, leaves brown on trees, and wind cries chilly in from the sea. The Change has come—the spinning wheel. Nothing lasts forever. And though they know it not, young Sarah and Daniel have but little time left together.

* * *

It is during one wet October night, when an old man limps awkwardly into the inn at Port Isaac, that Daniel's luck changes. The old wayfarer joins in at the table where Daniel, as usual, is winning. Daniel welcomes him openly. The Irishman is in high spirits—he's had a good week doing the type of work he enjoys, trenching and walling and such like, and tomorrow he is off back up to Haven Cove to see his beloved Sarah.

Not that there weren't a few lasses that had caught his eye here. But Daniel has reined himself in—Sarah is special, and she trusts him too. He smiles warmly across at the grizzled old cripple who now joins in their game.

This one has rare luck apparently; during the course of that evening, he empties the whole contents of Daniel's purse, and Daniel clambers back to his cot up in the farmstead with sore head and light pockets. He doesn't mind though, the old tramp looked like he needed all the help he could get—besides, he'd win the money back next week for sure.

So, feathers unruffled, Daniel borrows a week's wages in advance from the farmer, his employer. Next morning he rides back up to Haven Cove where Sarah is waiting for him.

But it turns out the old man who'd fleeced Daniel and friends at cards is something of a conniver. His name is Thomas Laity, he's an old soldier who'd survived the French wars, but got his legs blasted during the process. He'd boasted how as a wee drummer boy he'd seen old Bony brought low at Waterloo fields, over fifty years ago. Since that far off time, Old Tom's made a profession of limping into taverns and inns and seeking solace in the company of gentlefolk, and then stripping their purses bare while he cheats at card and dice.

As is the way of things, just a week after he'd left Port Isaac, Hobbling Tom passes through Trewenny's Cross on his way up to Stratton Town. He stops for the night. It is early and the inn is empty—so no chance to ply his trade just yet. So instead Tom settles his old bones by the fire, leans on his stave and dozes for a time.

As chance allows, on this very night one Robert Cutting decides to renew his former acquaintance at the 'Cross—deeming it now time enough for Big John to have forgiven him, and having become entirely weary of Thomas's brooding company all summer. Robert now seats himself close to old Tom, so as to share some of the fire's warmth. When Big John approaches the two with ale, Robert smiles up in friendly fashion.

"There won't be any trouble, John," Robert promises. "I've changed me ways."

"There had better not be, boyo," John replies, after awarding Robert a stern look to boot.

"That Irishman left—so I heard," Robert says cheerfully. Old Tom, still half dozing, lifts a lid hearing that.

"Aye—and for the best as it turns out," John says. "But don't you get too comfy, Master Robert. That lad was popular here—unlike some others I could name."

Robert shrugs, "I told you I've changed. I cannot speak for Thomas though." Big John shakes his head, and moves on to see to the barrels outside.

Old Tom yawns and stretches; he smiles mischievously. "Irishman—heh?" Tom says.

"What?" Robert sees no reason to converse with the bony old cripple aside of him.

"This Irish fella, perhaps he's the same young lad I was speaking to just last week," says Tom with a wink.

"What did he look like?" Robert's ears have picked up suddenly.

"Young, dark haired and black-eyed—comely looking lad, I'd say. And a ladies' man, I'd warrant too. Though a poor one—especially after I took all his coin at cards," Tom laughs at that.

"Where to?" Robert isn't laughing.

"Port Isaac—down in the harbour there," responds Tom, now enjoying the attention he is receiving from this local lad. "I recall now—Danny—that was the lad's name: said he had a girl up around these parts somewhere." Tom takes a long slow pull at his tankard and drains the contents, he winks at Robert.

"Thirsty work, all this talking, m' boy." Robert (unusually generous) orders him another. "Mentioned this very establishment—so he did. Reason why I called in." Hobbling Tom says this after thanking Robert for his ale—delivered again by Big John on a tray.

"Irishman say where he was staying when back here?" Robert demands.

"I'm not one for telling yarns, laddie." Tom winks at him again.

"I'll purchase you bottle a brandy—keep the chill off." Robert signals John across.

"Ah, well then." Big John gives Robert a suspicious look, but produces the clay flask of brandy for the old man, (who incidentally John doesn't much like the look of—John isn't enjoying the calibre of customer this evening but—needs must).

Hobbling Tom smiles his gap-toothy grin, as he sips the smooth brandy from the flask. "Aw, that's nice," Tom says. "Smooth."

"About this Irish fellow…" Robert presses.

"Ah, yes—him." Tom grins again. "Laddo was well into his cups the other night; said he regularly beds the best-looking maid in these here parts—Sarah he called her; he said she lives with her aunt by the sea. Mentioned he'd met her in this very establishment—as it happens. Strange coincidence that—don't you think lad? What—you off already, boy? Something I said?—I'm not one for gossip," chuckles Tom.

Robert, without further word, ups and leaves old Tom to gaily peruse the amber contents of his flask. The old boy grins across at John, who is watching Robert Cutting's hasty departure with a heavy frown.

"Good stuff, this," says Tom. Big John ignores him. "Strange lad, that one," Tom mutters to himself, and then nods sleepy by the fire again.

* * *

She senses their chosen hour approaching fast, feels sorrow at what shall come to pass—this game they play has no winners. She walks on, lost, her thoughts dreamy and drifting; her dress, as always, soaked by spray, and her copper hair wild and wind-lashed. She thinks about him as she always does at this hour: she misses him so much—the long cold wait has never lessened the pain she feels. Every day the same—hers is a lonely existence. Surely it was inevitable—she thinks. One day he will return.

What choice has she, but to wait upon that fateful tide?

She turns her back on the others; they are young yet—those two. And instead, the woman now watches the morning star brighten the horizon. She sees it wander free of the ocean's mantle. That star is her signal, announcing she must now depart for a time. She turns away, walks on as morning lightens the clouds to pinkish-grey. Beside her walks loyal sorrow—her constant companion these many days. He gently takes her hand, escorts her back along the beach. She turns one last time... feels the tear trace down her cheek. Inevitable...

Chapter 9

Mrs. Harrison

KATE DIALED AGAIN, BUT STILL Tony didn't pick up. She'd already left three messages since last night.

Damn you, Tony—he wasn't usually this unreliable. Kate threw her iPhone on the bed in disgust; two minutes later it responded by beeping a message and throbbing robustly. Kate pounced on it, punched the pass code in, and then retrieved the message. Tony—finally. She played it—no voice, nothing... just crackle.

Crap!

Kate dialed again: Tony's voice kicked in on his answer phone: *Hi... Tony here... I'll get back as soon as can... Thanks for calling...*

Shit!

Kate studied her watch—8.45 pm. Richard doubtless was still in the bar, or else moping like a love sick puppy down on the beach. She didn't care either way. Kate had had enough buffoonery from her husband to last a lifetime. Oh, sure—she could be short sometimes. And yes—Richard had been through it of late. So what? Shit happens.

Most times, Kate tolerated Richard—she'd loved him once, in her own way.

But that was then.

Her ardour had cooled; her passion congealed—as stale gravy left from yesterday's roast. Any affection she'd once felt was wearing thin, and as a couple they were positively threadbare.

Time to move on.

It all started going wrong when Richard lost his finance position. He'd been working opposite St Pauls Cathedral, and loved it. He'd stayed late on most evenings, beavering away industriously while the others had piled in the pub. Richard had been ambitious, back then.

Some of Kate's girlfriends suggested he had a lover. Kate had giggled hysterically at that.

What... Richard? They had laughed too, after thinking about what they had said. Richard Harrison didn't do sexy—never had. But at least back then he'd been kind and witty, and occasionally fun to be with. Nowadays it was like being hitched to Mr. Bean— needless to add, without the humour. Kate just couldn't fathom what was wrong with her husband; he'd lost all his confidence after losing that job.

So what—just a bloody job and so many others had fallen by the wayside, and some of Richard's friends among them too. But they hadn't acted like idiots, Kate suspected; men like Kevin Jones and Paul Hastings would dust themselves off, and get back on the horse. Not Richard Harrison. Richard was weak—that was one four letter word Kate despised.

He took it all too personal, did Richard. It was as though they were out to get him—just him—and it wasn't because of the biggest financial crisis in over half a century. He'd been so melodramatic. And then when she'd suggested he sell the TT, oh what a fuss he'd made—like a little boy whose spiteful brother had snapped the wing off one of his Airfix Spitfires. Yes, it had been a nice car—so what? Get another job, Richard Harrison, and then buy another car—simple.

And then she'd suggested Greece—she'd found a real bargain on Kos (just a week—nothing flash,) but stupid Richard had said they couldn't afford it, and instead suggested they come down here to this shit hole of fog, mist and rain instead. This trip would probably prove more expensive anyway—particularly after Kate exhausted her frustration on Truro high street again: nothing against Cornwall—but in November? And this Haven Hotel was like the scene from some sixties Hammer Horror set. Even the dreary locals in the bar looked like they had bit parts. This place wasn't Kate's scene—not at all. But there were other factors at play here.

But Kate had resignedly agreed, when Richard suggested they return here. Anything to stop his ceaseless carping. Let him think that anyway—Kate dare not reveal her agenda. Not until they had things sorted.

But Kate's curiosity had been raised by Richard's odd behaviour over the last two days—in fact, from the minute they had happened upon this haven of hospitality and sunshine. Kate had to face the facts—Richard Harrison was acting decidedly odd. Deliberate—she didn't think so. Richard was far too naive to be contriving. That was her department.

Richard claimed he was seeing things (a woman apparently—ha! hilarious that one.) Oh, and now the locals were splicing his whiskey, too. What utter tripe—why couldn't her husband just admit he'd gotten drunk, like any real man would. Kate would have forgiven that—she wouldn't have been pleased, but at least she'd know Richard was normal. Instead, he was Dick by name and Dick by nature. She, Kate, was married to a neurotic moron whose recent behaviour was some cause for concern. But was Kate concerned? Perhaps... but then again, perhaps not.

* * *

Kate dialed again. This time she left a peeved message: "Tony—it's Kate! Call me when you pick up. It's about Richard... we... need to talk. Soonest would be good."

An hour passed; no sign of her errant husband and no reply from Tony. Kate had had enough.

You win, Harrison.

When Kate entered the bar room, it was nearly empty—just the scruffy old guy with the estuary accent in the corner, that and a young couple cuddling and giggling at a nearby table. The sight of those two turned Kate's stomach. If people had to dribble over each other, then they should do it in private. Kate wasn't a prude, but she did believe in self respect. The two love birds evidently didn't—was that his tongue in her ear? Kate winced; she looked about. Richard was nowhere to be seen. Kate tapped her neat fingers; waited as the girl, Angela, (a nicer kid by far than the dour Morwenna,) passed her a glass of chilled lager and smilingly took her money.

"Any sign of my husband?" Kate asked, and after receiving a blank look added, "Mousey hair, going thin on top, middle height—likes Irish whiskey. Oh, and he apparently got quite drunk in here last night."

Angela smiled sympathetically. "My night off last night," she explained. Then a thought took her. "There was a guy sitting over by that window earlier." Angela pointed to the other end of the bar room where the table looked out on the sea. "He was reading some old book; seemed lost in his own little world. He had a few pints of Stoggs and then went outside—that sound like your bloke?"

"Oh, yeah."

Kate thanked Angela, and took her seat at the aforementioned table. Outside the night was clear and still. For a time Kate watched the sea's silver foam crash and spill into the pebbly cove below. A wan moon pierced the cloud. Kate managed a thin smile, seeing perhaps for the first time the raw beauty and enchantment of this place.

The lager softened her mood too. Perhaps she was being too hard on Richard? It was his mother's fault—Rebecca Harrison had indulged that boy of hers ever since his elder sister died in that awful car crash, seven years back.

Yes, Kate decided on reflection—maybe it was time to cut Richard some slack—perhaps then she would discover what was really going on inside that muddled head of his. But then—did that really matter after what she had decided? But Kate was curious, so yes, it would be good to know.

An hour passed; Kate waited, letting her agile thoughts go where they will. When her iPhone showed 22:35 hrs, Kate started to fret. What the hell was he doing out there all this time? And the weather was shifting again—Kate had never known such unreliable weather as they had witnessed down here. Even as Kate gazed out, fresh rain beaded the glass, and that awful wind returned with a vengeance to rattle the panes. Kate shivered, thinking of her stupid husband outside. Just then her phone throbbed on the table. Tony—at last!

Kate picked up. "Tony... I... we need to... *Tony?*"

Nothing. No bloody signal! Jesus, hadn't these people heard of Wi-Fi? Kate asked the girl, Angela, who replied that the signal came and went and that you got used to it—which didn't help Kate much.

To hell with you, Harrison—Kate purchased a large brandy and soda, and went back to her room. She called Tony—got through. Answer phone again. *Fuck the pair of you!*

Kate quite tipsy now—she wasn't much of a drinker—discarded her jeans and knickers on the bed and, (t-shirt and bra still intact), sprawled head first on the duvet. Within minutes she was sound asleep.

When Richard returned at three thirty, Kate never heard him. Neither did she witness the tall woman that followed him inside the room. Stored neatly in her jeans, the iPhone throbbed and hummed four times, finally subsiding sometime before dawn. Kate slept on, her dreams revealing nothing.

* * *

Some say natural arches are doorways opening upon other worlds. Portals where (at certain times of year and month,) those that passed beneath could find themselves whisked away into some other dimension, time or place. A few locals believed the sea-arch found just half a mile south of Haven Cove contained such mystic properties—though most sensible folk claimed such fanciful notions as just plain daft. Despite that, it was an eerie place to venture after dark. When the moon spilled silver on that weathered slate, it was possible to imagine any number of things.

And what we imagine can sometimes come true—more is hidden than found. Coincidence: a convenient word, it masks the infinitely subtle machinations of a higher force. A benign force? We like to think so. Certainly there are echoes out there we can never comprehend; nuances and suggestions, hints, rumours and signs—all waiting for those who know where to look.

And she is one such.

Among these echoes are cold things—dark zephyrs that would harm if they could. She now walking the night is one of these. She watches as her hunger grows. It is almost time.

Sea and surge and driving rain—and cold, cruel wind whistling stark through the arch's ancient portal! This is her place now—where she comes when she feels most lost. She is alone here—her malice keeps the other one away. She feels safe in this world between worlds, where time and space hold no power and meaning.

But here is an intruder—a man foolhardy enough to test the returning tide. But then, this too suits her well. He is expected, after all.

She studies the man's approach and shows her rotten-tooth smile. This one's curiosity will prove his downfall. She sees him stumble on a rock and then clamber froglike back to his feet; a fool certainly.

The moon rides out—she sees the fervour in his eyes. Time to play. She shows herself to him as he gazes spellbound up at the glistening arch. She notes how his trainers and jeans are soaked by wave and spume, and his thinning hair matted and dishevelled. But he doesn't see her this time, and turns away; her prey starts slowly trudging back, slipping and tripping on the wet uneven rocks. Fool indeed.

Ravenous for what he can give her, the woman follows behind in eager silence. The tide is coming in fast now and the man has to hurry, lest he gets cut off.

He gains the beach, and stands puffing and shaking for a minute before regaining his momentum. Pale shadow, she is close behind him now, and he still unaware of her presence. He staggers up wet and weary to the old hotel; she follows close behind. He turns the latch and ventures inside. Again, she follows.

* * *

The lounge is empty: the only sound is the wind outside. Richard makes for the stairs, sourcing his room-key after a minute's drunken fumbling. He turns it; enters their room. Richard, soaked and freezing, strips naked and tosses his wet garments on the floor. He towels himself off in the bathroom, yawns twice, and then collapses onto the bed and commences snoring enthusiastically in Kate's ear.

The dark haired woman now watches in the corner. She waits for the moon, her ally, and then once he is with her, she silently slides the rusty knife free of its hiding place, deep inside her tattered gown. She fingers its length with her broken nails. Soon... Just one more night—the moon would be full tomorrow and only then could *he* come. It was only fair for *him* to partake. Together they would perform their bloody deed. But tonight, let them sleep easy—she can wait and has many things to prepare. So she leaves the sleeping bodies and fades back into the shadows of the night. Tomorrow, everything would change. In just a few hours, she and her lover will be free. And they had waited so very long for this.

Chapter 10

A Bloody Deed

DANIEL URGES THE PONY UP the hill. It is hard to see through the fret and mist. It is early November—he's finished at the farm now and is back to re-join Sarah and Susan at the cottage. He has done well, has Daniel. The farmer, Jonathan, likes him and has promised him more work next spring—should he wish it. Daniel likes Port Isaac—he has friends there now, and some of the girls... well, if it wasn't for sweet Sarah...?

Sweet, lovely Sarah—she who he would be with again in just an hour or so! Daniel spurs his mare on, but the way is muddy and her progress very slow. To his left he hears the rumour of sea on stone, whilst at his right a shoulder of moor looms dark and sullen.

He rides on, carefully urging his steed over bog-grass and tangled tussock. The moorland is treacherous this time of year, and patience is needed to cross. At last, Daniel enters a copse at the moor's northern fringe, a deep fold cutting down midst shrub and briar. Daniel leans back in the saddle, commences steering the pony between stubby wild oaks and battered creaking ash. The path is narrow here; the way ahead and down strewn with loose rock and seeping water. But he is nearly home!

Daniel smiles when an orange fox cuts urgent across his path, and above his head a crow takes flight, mocking horse and rider with its rasping calls. The trees close in—dark sentries dripping mist and murk.

A noise behind him.

Daniel turns, looks back, just as the mare's fore-hoof steps on the trap and it closes wickedly upon her. The mare buckles—tosses her rider from his saddle.

Daniel thuds hard into wet rocky soil; he rolls on impact, but his shoulder is dislocated and his arm badly broken. He stands groaning.

A man blocks his way.

Daniel recognises Thomas Cutting, smiling and gripping his cudgel.

Fuck you!

Daniel lashes out with his good fist, but misses as Thomas steps aside. A blow numbs the back of his skull, Robert smiles as he frees the trap from the pony's leg. It isn't broken—why waste a good animal? Robert swings out again, hitting Daniel hard across the back of his head.

Daniel stumbles; he curses; spits bloody phlegm up into Thomas's beaming face. Thomas kicks him hard in the groin, and, as Daniel falls forward, Thomas rams his stave's fire-hardened tip into the face of his rival, breaking Daniel's jaw.

Daniel slumps; he tries to rise but Thomas's boot slams hard into the back of his head. Then the brothers are upon him, their heavy sticks beating and thudding until Daniel's blood seeps into the mulchy damp earth, and he crumples and lies still. The wood watches in silence, the birds too outraged to speak. Daniel Flannigan is dead.

Murder, cold and bloody, up there on the moor

* * *

They carry Daniel's body back up the track to the open moorland. After making sure no one is about, the brothers drag the limp corpse the hundred yards or so over to the high cliff edge. After getting their breath back, they toss him over. Robert laughs as Daniel's broken body cartwheels down, colliding with rock and stone, until he is lost in the wild wash of winter water. Thomas just smirks. Then after a few minutes gloating, the two then repair hastily back to their farm, both well content and satisfied with how their day has gone.

* * *

They find Daniel's body washed up on Haven Cove, his once fine features all bloated and fishy-rotten. Susan weeps, but Sarah says nothing. Later that night, she takes herself up upon the Long Cliff. There Sarah stands alone, her eyes wild; still no tear dare moisten her cheek. She is fey. Her mind is gone. She stands there— a ragged figure, her body buffeted and her dress torn and tattered. Sarah listens to the cold wind, as he cries out the name of her beloved, now lost.

Daniel, Daniel, Daaaaniel...

Here Sarah stands poised and brittle, feeling no chill as evening darkens into night. A gaunt silhouette framed by starry night and cliff edge.

And Sarah jumps...

Her pale body plummets silent down through winter's night; her dress, like torn sailcloth, flaps behind her and beside her. And, as Sarah tumbles and flops, the angry wind rides with her, his cold voice shrieking out her lover's name. She sees the water racing up to greet her: Sarah smiles and closes her eyes.

Daniel—I am coming...

* * *

Daniel Flannigan is buried in the church amidst the ancient oaks, but Sarah's body isn't found. Big John leads the search for her, even Joe Collins is there. But Sarah, they don't find. She is now feared lost to wave and ocean.

But when a while later a girl's headless body is washed up dry by the incoming tide at Wide Mouth Bay, tongues start wagging. Rumour claims this is one Sarah Hosking, lately of Trewenny's Cross—having been lost to that parish a little while back. It is, however, impossible to be certain as there was only one witness claiming to have seen the girl's corpse. This was a local fisher's wife. A woman well respected—both practical and sensible. Not one for fanciful notions. And yet her tale is strange.

Story goes, when the fishwife finds the dead girl's body she seeks assistance, returning a short time later with two strong men to drag the corpse ashore. But the body has gone. This they find decidedly queer, as the tide has since retreated back a good way from when the woman had found her, almost an hour ago. The fishermen curse this waste of their time; they shake their heads and leave the beach muttering.

The woman ignores them, staying put a moment longer, she is puzzled by this, and edgy. Then something catches her eye. She stoops uneasy—looks closer and her heart turns to stone.

There is something written in the sand at her feet. Just one scratchy word, its letters faint and fading fast as the wintry sun bleaches out their creases. The woman has scarce glimpsed it before the writing vanishes from view. She doubts her senses—perhaps she is unwell, she thinks. But surely she had seen it written there? Just one small word scraped softly into the cloggy sand.

Daniel.

The woman shivers and tugs at her shawl—it is bitter out here on the beach alone. She wipes a salty tear from her wind-cold cheek and then turns, briskly walks away.

* * *

A month later, Master Joe Collins, slow of wit but kind of heart, is riding through the frosty track leading up to Long-cliff moor. He spies the trap discarded aside the road and deems it odd. That night, Joe reports his discovery to Big John, who also deems it strange. The very next day, John Nichols and Joe Collins walk up to the woody spot where Joe found the trap. John tuts and scratches his beard as he fumbles the length of the snare.

"Queer is this," Big John says, recognising the trap, having seen its like before. "And yet—familiar, heh Joe?"

Joe nods. "Looks like one of Robert Cutting's traps," he says—pleased with himself for recognising the rude design cut into the object. "It's a long way from Treliggan, int it, John?"

Big John grins. "You're a bright lad Joe," he says. "I'm thinking we had best alert the constable—what say you?" Joe agrees this is a good idea.

* * *

A week later: Robert Cutting is hauled in front of the magistrate at Bodmin Town. He is found wanting, but released after pleading insanity and enforced collusion; Robert is spared rope and gaol, and allowed to return home. It is apparent to all he is simple, thus blameless. It was Thomas they wanted—everyone.

Robert doesn't last though—his guilt eats into him. It were Master Joseph Collins as finds poor Robert Cutting hanging from the crossbeam of his hay barn one late February morning.

But crafty Thomas has sprung the trap, leaving his younger brother to soak up both guilt and retribution. Thomas is a survivor: he fares to up to London Town.

They now say that, once he reached the city, Thomas Cutting changed his name and profession. Rumours abound that he even had a family. But the Justice caught him at the end, and Master Thomas swung.

It was a hard grey morning when Thomas Cutting met his fate, an east wind cut brutal through those avids who watched on goggle-eyed. Susan Hosking was one such gathered at that hostile meeting. She'd kept her wits over the years and studied the lists of the condemned, hence when Thomas was apprehended she'd been ready and journeyed up. They say Susan, alone of those eager watchers gathered close in the chill, smiled when the rope snapped taut beneath dancing Thomas's head. There were none there as offered to tug hard at his feet—this was a murderer, so it was said. They also say Thomas enthusiastically swung to and fro, and kicked out for a time. But then the hangmen oft rigged the ropes so the crowd had more of a show.

Chapter 11

Disclosure

RICHARD HAD READ THE PASSAGE over and over, whilst sitting at the table with beer close by and whiskey gripped in shaking hands. It read thus:

In the mid/late nineteenth century at a quiet cove south of Stratton Town, a young girl's body was found washed up on the shore at Widemouth Bay. Though the body was lost to the sea again before formal identification, it was believed this poor soul had jumped from one of the high cliffs looming above the nearby cove known simply as Haven.

Unrecognisable, she was rumoured to be one Sarah Hosking, an eighteen year old local girl who had worked for some while at nearby Trewenny's Cross. There, it is said, this Sarah met a charming young Irishman who was staying at the inn while he worked on farms in the locality. These two had taken a rare fancy to each other, but their bliss had been bitterly brief, for the Irish lad had been murdered by a jealous local. The eldest of two brothers who—it transpired later—had been seeking Sarah's affections for quite some time. After her lover's murder, the distraught, inconsolable Sarah had taken to strolling up to the high cliff. There in despair, Sarah Hosking had jumped to her ruin on a wild windy night in early November 1868.

A certain Robert Cutting was found hanging from a crossbeam in a cattle barn at nearby farm Treliggan Corners, some time later. This Robert had ended his own life as a result of the guilt and shame he apparently felt after Sarah's sad demise. However, it was rumoured that his older brother, Thomas Cutting, was the real perpetrator of the crime. Due to a strange quirk of fate, the Peelers eventually caught up with this Thomas many years later. He had fled to London where, after changing his name, Thomas Cutting had procured successful employment as a grave digger. They say he married, and fathered three children. Thomas was hanged at Tyburn Hill in early 1886.

It was fascinating, and yet quite why he was so obsessed with the story baffled Richard. Certainly he was spooked, but in an odd way relieved too. He wasn't losing the plot (thank God), but rather was being stalked (haunted for certain) by the ghost of a long dead girl. Though the woman he'd seen on the beach appeared in her forties—so that made little sense either.

But Richard's instinct screamed at him that they were the same: the stranger on the beach, the women in his dream last night, and this long dead girl, Sarah Hosking.

But what was the connection with him? Perhaps she hated all men and lurked angry in the corridors of the Haven Hotel, or else out there on the beach. It was a riddle, but one at last he could relax about. He wasn't a nutter—just someone caught up in other peoples' shit. Nothing new there—except that this particular person was dead. Long dead.

That evening, Richard got drunk again. He shunned the locals—the bar was almost deserted tonight, so that was easy. At half eight, he took to strolling outside again. Some weird compulsion had propelled Richard to the left side of the cove—the tide was coming in now, but there was plenty of room for walking between crashing wave and shadowy rock.

Richard, drunk and dreamy, must have ventured for half a mile when he saw the arch looming out of the dark. An impressive sight, it nevertheless gave him the shivers. Déjà vu—an odd tingle creeping along his spine; it had made Richard shiver.

I know this place... I've been here at some other time.

Richard laughed then. He was drunk and star-gazey was all, and then a sudden blast of icy rain in his face reminded Richard that it was getting quite late, and the tide was lapping in close to his feet. Best he sober up, and quickly too. Richard turned to start making his way back, but had only walked a couple of yards before he stopped for a moment.

Someone's watching me under that arch.

Richard turned around, looked back at the sea arch; the shoulder of rock where the arch's pillar met the ground was now assaulted by the white fury of returning wave. There was no one there—just his imagination again. But Richard was spooked; he picked up his pace, tripped and fell, got up and slipped again. Eventually Richard made it back to his room, soaked and edgy, and all the time feeling someone watching him. He woke sometime before dawn, beside him Kate snored (unusual for her.) Richard yawned and closed his eyes. Within minutes, he was sound asleep.

* * *

Kate slept in, whilst Richard went for a stroll before breakfast. He felt okay this morning, which was surprising after the booze he'd put away last night. Richard decided not to dwell on his obsession with the woman on the beach and his suspicions concerning her identity.

Instead, he focussed on full English (served up by 'happiness is' Morwenna.) Kate joined him and proposed another run into Truro. Richard had no problem with that, so they left an hour later.

This trip proved less tense than the last. Kate seemed relaxed today, and that helped Richard relax too. He steered well away from book shops, instead he checked out the latest tablets in the gadget store, before venturing on to the DVD department.

Kate caught him brooding outside Marks; she was all smiles this lunchtime—her arms laden with bags of various sizes and shapes. Her quest had obviously proved fruitful, and Kate Harrison was never happier than when she was spending money (money they didn't have, Richard couldn't help thinking.)

Oh well...

Kate ignored Richard's gaunt expression; she suggested they go eat, and then wind back along the north coast taking the scenic route. It was a fine winter's day. The sun was out, and it was surprisingly warm for this late in the year. Richard shrugged a weary yes.

That drive seemed to go on forever, in Richard's opinion. Though Kate was soaking in the stunning scenery, he was itching to get back to their hotel and ask some piquant questions. He suspected the po-faced Morwenna knew something, and some of the others too. He needed answers; it was their last night tonight, and Richard wanted some satisfaction before returning to London—if only to assay his curiosity. Aside from that, he wanted to report the idiots who had laced his drinks. So Richard stewed in silence as Kate navigated sweeping bends, fending off all manner of tractors and trucks in her coastal sojourn.

A few miles south of their destination, Kate coolly angled the Jimny into a muddy pull-in that awarded a majestic view of sea and rocky outcrops. A few yards ahead, a battered sign read:

'Waterfall and holy well.'

Beneath those words, a faded arrow hinted toward a track leading on down into distant rook-noisy trees. "Oh look, a waterfall, Richard!" Kate was already outside the car. "Let's go see."

Richard muttered that he'd rather get back to the hotel and take a shower. He couldn't understand why his wife was so chirpy today. Almost she seemed happy to be here, in Cornwall with him—Richard. He pulled a face.

"To the bar, you mean," laughed Kate. "Come on, the walk

will do you good, Harrison. It'll burn off some of that fat you've acquired of late."

"I've already walked miles through Truro." Richard's moan fell on deaf ears. Kate walked on, brisk and bright. Richard trudged behind, scowling at the back of his wife's blue sports anorak, as she threaded her way down the track into the dense canopy of trees.

Cheerful bitch... The last thing Richard needed right now was a bloody wood walk with some doubtless 'tiny' waterfall at its conclusion. He felt tired and edgy—the drink and late night now taking their toll. And just why was Kate so damned perky this afternoon?

The walk took longer than Kate had expected—not that she cared. Kate loved the woods in winter, unlike Richard who usually stayed well clear from anything with bark on it. She'd dragged him to a garden centre once to look at roses; Richard had been bored stiff. He didn't do foliage—he was more into motor racing and football, than wildlife and flowers. He viewed gardening as being the domains of the 'pipe and slippers brigade'—something he'd be forced into when he was old and fat, and could no longer escape to the pub for sanctuary.

This wood was beautiful, though—he had to admit that. The trees clung stubbornly to the odd brown leaf (though most were long gone now,) and the path at their feet was mulched with a sweet mould-smelling carpet of birch, oak and ash. Richard managed a smile despite himself.

The sun patrolled high above, casting golden shafts of light that flickered and glistened between the woody labyrinth of branch and bough. The path passed a wishing well with a saint's name written beside it.

Here they stopped briefly, while Kate launched a twenty pence piece into the dull blackness within the well's perimeter. Further on, the path descended down to a rock-strewn stream, which gurgled and chimed as they walked alongside it. Ahead was a boggy glade, bathed with sunlight and framed with old crack-willows that creaked and groaned in the slight chilling breeze.

Richard felt his gaze drawn to that glade, and weirdly, he

felt a sudden pang of guilt together with a profound feeling of déjà-vu—again.

I know this place.

Kate's shout announced the waterfall's presence ahead, but Richard hardly heard her. Instead he saw the naked pale skin of a woman's body, as she rolled beneath her dark haired lover in the dewy mantle, just yards in front of where he was standing. The moment passed—the briefest glimmer—but he had seen her there clear as the day.

The waterfall was very familiar too, as were the strange little rags dangling from the willow trees surrounding the wide clear basin at its feet.

"It's so beautiful," marvelled Kate. "Enchanting. Kind of mysterious too, don't you think? Like something out of a fairy tale." Her eyes locked on the rags. "What are those things?"

"They're called jowds in these parts," Richard replied. He didn't have a clue why he knew that—he just did. It was just another coincidence, he told himself. He must have read it somewhere. Perhaps in the goblin book.

"I'm impressed," Kate answered, "It's all very... Arthurian—if that's the right word." They had passed close to Tintagel—Kate had wanted to look at the castle, but Richard hadn't. When Richard didn't respond, Kate looked across to where he was standing, stooped and haggard. She caught his odd expression, and her lip twitched.

"Richard, I'm getting worried about you," Kate said. "You've been acting very strange since we came on this trip. Whatever is the matter?"

"I'm just tired, Kate," he responded lamely. "I told you, I hardly slept the other night when those arseholes laced my whiskey." Kate refused to be drawn back into that one.

"Besides," Richard added, "this place gives me the willies. God only knows what people got up to here in past times."

"You're such a townie," said Kate, but she was feeling tired now too. "Come on then, let's get back—it'll be dark in an hour or so," Kate said.

Once again she led the way. Kate glanced back at her husband several times as they walked. If she was worried about him, she didn't show it, enduring his woeful expressions with cheerful indifference.

But both felt relieved when they reached the car. Especially since the rain had pounced on them just as they cleared the trees. The sun, now smothered by dark cloud, showed no promise of return, and a harsh wind hurled cold droplets of wintry rain down upon them as they half trotted and slipped the last hundred yards. It now felt like November.

Richard sniffled as he opened the car door, whilst Kate threw her soaked anorak on the back seat and fired the engine. Richard remained glum as Kate, glimpsing the road ahead between the scraping wipers, drove on.

I'm catching a cold. Hardly surprising, Richard thought, after sneezing theatrically—it would probably develop into swine flu, the way his luck was running of late. He sneezed again, questing for sympathy. He received none; Kate ignored him.

As Kate cleared Boscastle, Richard found his mind wandering back to the old book and its revealing contents. He now suspected this Daniel person was the girl Sarah's murdered lover—it would explain why the ghost was so pissed off. But he hadn't killed poor old Daniel, so why take it out on him? Or had he? A sudden chill cut knife-sharp into Richard's guts.

Oh stop this!

It was all his imagination working overtime—again. He was stressed, tired and morose, and tomorrow would be heading back up to London—thank goodness. Besides, the woman he had seen on the beach had looked nearly forty. Sarah Hosking had only been eighteen. There was no connection—couldn't be. Or could there?

He had another ghastly thought. Perhaps she was another ghost, and this Daniel geezer a third? Maybe there was a whole gang of them loitering on that beach? A ghost convention. Richard made a funny noise, and Kate awarded him a quizzical eye.

"You alright?"

"Fine."

But he was far from alright. Richard needed answers—and before they left in the morning. Richard was convinced those sods at the hotel had deliberately kept him in the dark, and that girl Morwenna wasn't the sort to let on—probably gave them that room because she knew it was haunted. It was obvious that Morwenna hadn't much time for Richard—or Kate, for that matter. Well, he would have curt words with the lot of them this evening. He'd turn the joke back on them. Tonight, Richard told himself as Kate glided the Jimny into the car park, he would discover the truth behind young Sarah Hosking and her murdered lover.

* * *

Bugger this traffic—he was late already! The elevated section was heaving tonight; Tony fussed at the dials on the radio as his Porsche inched passed the London Arc. He couldn't decide between Capital and Heart FM. He settled for Heart and smiled as the sultry voice of Toni Tennille soothed his fraying nervous system.

Tony was in deep shit this morning. This would be the third time he'd been late for a meeting in as many weeks. Tony blamed Richard Harrison wholly for that. The guy was a useless dick. Kate deserved better.

He cut across into the middle lane as a truck loomed up behind him. Kate had been desperate to get hold of him yesterday—something was wrong clearly, something that concerned her stupid husband. No doubt about that.

He'd tried to get hold of Kate five times through the night. Tony hadn't spoken to her in four days and was missing her company more than he should be. Oh, he wasn't worried about dickhead Richard—but if Cassie found out about him and Kate—(not to mention the kids) he would be right up shit alley.

Fuck it! Tony fumbled with his iPhone and dialed Kate's number. Answer phone. *Pick up Kate, for Christ sake*! Nothing.

The woman behind awarded him her horn, and Tony gave her the finger; *fuck this,* he spun the wheel; the Porsche screeched across to the hard shoulder. From there Tony undercut the crawling traffic as he sped towards South Ken, car horns blaring and headlights flashing bright behind him. He'd get this bloody meeting over with, and then get hold of Kate.

Cornwall—bloody Richard again. What arsehole takes his wife to Cornwall in November? Half hour later, Tony landed the Porsche like a missile in the vacant parking lot. He jumped out, pressed the remote and, after straightening his tie, hurried up to the conference room. Once there, Tony made his excuses, and then smilingly joined in with the other bullshitters.

* * *

Kate retained her good spirits that night, and actually spent several hours with him at the bar; (if only to ensure that he wasn't drinking too much.) She turned in around nine thirty to watch some thriller on Sky. Richard pecked her cheek and grinned.

Yes darling—I'll be good.

Richard claimed a redundant barstool and perched happily. Half hour passed, Richard sat dreaming and drinking, his eyes misting over. Occasionally he grinned at Morwenna, (who for her part ignored him except when he required replenishment—which was not infrequent.)

Richard ordered a sly whiskey along with his fifth lager. He'd promised Kate he wasn't going to touch the stuff again. But to hell with it, he was on vacation, wasn't he? Richard, not convinced by that word, needed all the help he could get at the moment—and the blessed Bushmills slipped down the throat so damned easy. He drained the double and, still grinning stupidly, ordered another from the charming Morwenna.

The Haven Hotel was quiet tonight, but not dead like it had been yesterday. There were a few 'surf dudes' crouched around a pool game, and a polite young couple sitting at a table to his right, watching the night rain bead the window panes in time with the beat of the three-tune juke box, way over in the corner. There was no sign of the idiots that had fixed Richard's drinks, much to his annoyance. Richard was determined to have words with those boys before he left tomorrow morning. Morwenna (still ignoring him,) slouched comfy into a chair at the other end of the bar; she yawned, as she fingered her way through the gossip column of a month-old glossy mag.

"Anything about ghosts in that?" Richard called across, in a voice that was probably too loud, but he didn't care, fortified as he was by fine Irish liquor.

Morwenna gaped at him.

"What?" she asked, scratching her left earring and pulling a face.

"Ghosts—you know things that go bump in the night, or should I say *hotel room*." Richard shot her a blatant smile.

"I don't believe in ghosts," answered Morwenna. She hurriedly returned her gaze to the magazine. Richard noticed she looked uncomfortable, as she tried to hide her freckly features behind the pages.

"They exist," pressed Richard—his voice still too loud. "And I've seen one recently."

"So?" The girl rolled her eyes and fidgeted. But there was no escaping this creep. Resigned, Morwenna relented; she feigned shallow interest. "Where to?" Morwenna asked wearily.

"Out on the beach," replied Richard, grinning at her obvious discomfort. "And upstairs, Morwenna, in this very hotel." Richard was enjoying himself now. "I saw *her* last night—in my room."

"Who's *her?*" Morwenna's voice had gone quiet; her face paled a shade.

"Sarah Hosking." Richard was enjoying this now.

"Don't know who you mean."

Before Richard could press his advantage, a group of thirty-somethings entered the bar room. Morwenna, relieved by this timely intervention, hurried to serve them all drinks. She steered well clear of Richard for the rest of that night, which suited him well enough.

Towards eleven, the bar room filled and Richard, well on his way yet again, found himself sitting in his corner at the end of the bar, people watching, and dreaming contentedly into the depth of his glass. His heart missed a beat when a strong hand shook his shoulder. Angry, Richard looked up.

"You'll stir up trouble." The voice was a soft Cornish brogue, and it belonged to the youngish man that had been sitting at the table with his wife or girlfriend earlier. He was frowning down at Richard in an unfriendly manner, and it was evident that he too had drunk more than he should.

"What's the matter with you?" Richard glared back. He didn't care a jot that this bloke was bigger than him and had the build of a prop forward. Richard was armoured with whiskey, and both his shoulders were chipped tonight.

Just let him start...

"People like you," continued the rugby player," come down from 'up country' with lots of cash and lots of mouth." Just then, the girlfriend appeared and nudged the gorilla's shoulder.

"Josh, leave it," she urged. "He didn't mean any trouble. Come on now, you've got work in the morning." Josh glared at Richard for a moment longer and then slunk toward the door, glowering at anyone in his range. The girlfriend stayed put for a while.

"Locals around here don't mention that name," she said to Richard in a quiet voice. "It brings bad luck and gets people's backs up."

"But that's just stupid superstition," countered Richard.

The girlfriend shook her head. "That name is cursed as are two others—were I you I'd leave this place, mate. Go back to London, you're not welcome here." Without waiting for Richard's response, the girlfriend slid between the crowd now busy lining the bar, and quietly rejoined her hulking beau by the door. Together they awarded Richard a final venomous glare, before departing out into the cold drizzle of the November night.

Sod you too...

Richard waved a nonchalant hand at their departure, and then shouted Morwenna for another whiskey. He'd lost count by now and was past caring. On a whim he sought out the redundant cigarette machine by the toilets and, in sheer rebellion, purchased twenty B&H. Richard hadn't smoked for three years. Kate would kill him tomorrow, but he didn't care about that either. He filched a box of matches from the fireplace in the lounge and merged out into the gloom, armed with whiskey and smokes. He felt light-headed and giddy (even slightly sick), as the heady rush of nicotine surged through his veins.

Bugger them all, I'm going to get to the bottom of this.

Richard sat for a time on the wall that hedged the seaward side of the lane. A slate bulwark, it skirted the pebbly circumference of the cove. A ghost wall—Richard laughed—built to keep the spookies at bay. Not that that had worked recently. Richard could see nothing but gloom through the drizzly dark; perhaps *she* wasn't out there tonight. He yearned to see her again, and yet dreaded it too.

Why were women so complex—even astral ones? They were like cats—capricious and quirky. Even Kate, (a straightforward enough girl), had her peculiarities. Blokes are simple, thought Richard—they get drunk, fart and snore... but women?

Richard shrugged magnanimously to his imaginary audience, and waved his glass about in consternation. He had never really understood the fairer sex. He wasn't blessed with good looks or a glib tongue, so when Kate came along—well, he'd been a happy bunny, had our Richard. But this Cornish stay had proved an odd affair—Richard felt different than he had before—almost he was someone else, someone confident and strong. But then, perhaps that was the whiskey talking.

Eventually, Richard retired from his poignant vigil and returned inside. Ignoring the stragglers left in the bar, Richard shuffled wearily upstairs to the room. Kate, of course, was fast asleep, at least the curtains were drawn this time. Richard, exhausted and very drunk, staggered into his night shorts and flicked the light switch. Within seconds he was sound asleep.

Chapter 12

Retribution

TYBURN 1886. A LONE FIGURE stoops weary on the scaffold. It is cold and bleak—hail and wind batter him, but he feels nothing, is hollow inside.

Retribution.

He'd gone too far—he realises that now. And he had always known they would find him in the end—despite years of self-delusion.

Guilt will out, after all.

It would be hard for Kitty and the twins, and poor little Robert (named after his long dead brother.) He recoils as an egg—rotten and green—explodes into his face. Another strikes his shoulder and two more sail over his head. Then something hard thuds into his chest and he stumbles—almost falls (cheering and laughter down below.) Someone shouts close by, and the missiles stop coming. His ribs hurt and his back aches—the icy wind cuts into his bones, and his freezing hands are blue and numb, the cruel cord cutting deep into his flesh, and his arms pulled painfully tight behind his back. None of that mattered, though.

Guilt will out...

He'd been so careful, had Thomas: stayed out of their reach—just that stupid mistake had got him in the end.

Inevitable—truth will out...

As winter buffets his unshaven face, Thomas looks back in time. He sees the Irishman lying bloodied and still, and again imagines sweet Sarah Hosking crying out his name in hatred, before she plunges to her ruin from that dreadful cliff top.

I will haunt your nights forever, Cutting... her voice in the wind... everywhere.

And she had. That pale lost face had stayed with him these nineteen years.

If only he could turn back time. Thomas recalls hearing of Robert's death in the newspaper that day, and another lance of guilt loosens his bowels. He'd not returned to Cornwall, but had made a life for himself here in London Town, putting the past behind—and indeed, as a grave digger, burying it deep beneath the soil. He'd married cheerful Kitty, (what she'd seen in him Thomas never understood.) He'd loved her in his way, the children too. Thomas had changed utterly since that earlier time, he'd become a devout worshipper and upright citizen—shunning gin and ale. Almost, he believed he would never be caught, but it was Thomas himself that placed the noose around his neck.

Retribution—guilt will out in time. Inevitable...

He'd changed his name back then, and his identity. But Thomas couldn't banish the guilt or shame of his violent past. Truth will out indeed.

He blinks, sees the shouting throng gathered like storm-crows below—nothing like a good hanging to set the city folk a-nattering.

Thomas shudders, as they pull the hood down hard over his sweaty wet face; he cries out as the rough hemp tightens painfully around his neck.

"I'm sorry for what I did back then!" Thomas's voice is hoarse and muffled beneath the stifling hood. He hears the crowd hoot and jeer. The wind is shrieking all around him: he hears *her* voice

—*Time to die, Thomas Harrison...*

The trap drops: Thomas falls. The rope cuts hard into his neck—but Thomas is strong, and his neck doesn't break. He swings there amid the laughs, kicking out like a mad fool—his hidden face blackened with agony as he slowly suffocates. Thomas kicks and chokes, until at last the darkness takes him. But that is no escape: she is there—waiting with the bloody knife in hand.

Daniel...

* * *

Richard woke with a jolt. Outside, the full moon traced the edge of the curtains with eerie silver, and the distant surge of sea washed the sand clean nearby. It was very chilly in the room; cold and silent. Richard turned toward Kate and noticed she was missing.

He was alone in the bed! Kate's case was missing too—it had been over by the door when he'd come in—he vaguely recalled registering that fact.

She's gone—why?

Richard, blearing eyed and mouth stinking of fags and whiskey, threw the covers aside and gaped about naked in the room.

"Kate... Kate?" Richard pulled the drapes back—it was impossible to discern whether it was late or early, and he had no idea how long he'd been asleep. He felt like shit, but that was no indication. Richard gawped out at the car park below, easily visible under the moon's weird glow. No Jimny. Surprise, surprise.

Bitch... she must have been planning this all along.

Richard staggered across to the wash basin. He rinsed his face, farted noisily, and then stumbled clumsy into his jeans.

"You bitch!" Richard threw on a T-shirt and denim jacket, and made angrily for the door.

It was only then that Richard saw the note. He reached down to grip the paper, but shivered when he didn't recognise the hand.

Kate didn't write this... then who...?

Richard's body began to tremble and shake. He felt cold and sick, on the verge of freaking out. He fumbled for his reading glasses and studied the note; stained paper—torn and faded, and the ink barely legible. This was old. Hands now shaking uncontrollably, Richard gripped the parchment. Eyes straining, he read the scratchy words.

Here lieth the body of one Thomas Harrison of Battersea manor: hanged on this day for foulest murder—may God have mercy on his wicked soul.

Thomas Harrison—his great great grandfather had been hanged at Tyburn hill. Richard recalled how his dad had spooked him with that chilling tale when he was a kid.

I can't stand this..!

Richard threw the note on the floor, and without a backwards glance left the empty room behind. The face in the mirror watched his departure with a smile.

It is time...

She follows then, and then the other one too.

* * *

Five hours of sleet and howling wind, and with him driving at full pelt the whole bloody way! Tony, despite feeling shattered, couldn't wait to see her. At last! He pulled up at the lay-by around 4.30 am—Kate's blue Jimny now clearly visible beneath the bright moonlight. Tony slammed the Porsche's door shut, and ran across to greet her.

They hugged, kissed, and grinned at each other.

"I've missed you, darling," Kate said. "Where have you been... I tried to get hold of you days ago."

"I was tied up with crap," said Tony. "You know how that place is." He kissed her again—long and hard. "Does shit-for-brains suspect anything?"

"Nothing—innocent as a lamb." Kate winked at her long-time lover.

"To the slaughter, then," added Tony and laughed at his own wit. "So it's all as we planned," he said.

"Just so," responded Kate, and kissed him again. "But we need to get moving before first light. You remember the place, Tony?"

"Of course—I'm hardly likely to forget that, Kate."

"True."

Minutes later, Tony tucked his Porsche neatly behind Kate's

jeep as she steered her vehicle back down through the shadowy lanes. When they reached the beach, dark clouds rolled in from the west, and squally rain battered the windscreens of both cars. Tony cursed the weather again, but there was nothing for it—they had to get this done.

Chapter 13

Daniel

RICHARD WRENCHED THE BOLT BACK, and floundered out into the night. He had no idea where he was going, he felt irrational and distraught. Kate had left him without even a word. He staggered down the steps and, without thinking, found himself back on the empty beach. Richard shivered as a wall of cloud swallowed the moon. He walked on, desolate, as the wind picked up and sudden hail hammered his face.

What am I doing?

It was raw and bleak, and Richard's world had fallen apart. He felt desperate... lost. He staggered toward the greyness of murmuring water ahead, sobbing and muttering...

Bitch, bitch, bitch...

A shadow blocked his way: Richard recognised her in an instant—those drawn features and huge violet eyes and that wanton, hungry expression. She was smiling at him, bidding him follow her along the strand.

And Richard followed—what else could he do? Kate had left him, but *she* still wanted him. And he wanted her—needed her.

Sarah...!

* * *

He waits beneath the sea-arch as his love leads the sacrifice on toward him. Thomas is much changed—but then so are they all. Daniel smiles as she leads him on—the groping weakling fool, so different from back then. He grips the rock in his right hand, and readies himself. Sarah sees her lover waiting there, and nods toward him. Daniel slides behind the arch's column and counts slowly as she brings him into reach. Sarah passes beneath the arch, just as the full moon rides free from cloud and weirdly lights their passage. Sarah walks through smiling, and this new weaker Thomas is right behind her. Daniel grins wolfishly. He winks at Sarah.

At last!

He grips the rock and swings down hard.

* * *

Richard sprawled as the heavy blow cracked open his head; he tried to stand but someone held him pinned from behind.

What's this...?

She stood before him then—the woman, the other woman— the cruel one in the mirror. Her hair sleek and black, jet black— why had he not noticed that before? Or had he? And those eyes... *Sarah?*

Like violets...

Richard screamed when he saw the rusty knife clutched tight in her pale right fist.

Please... no!

Richard struggled, but to no avail. A strong hand covered his mouth; forced his head back hard.

Please—NO!

Sarah slices the knife deep along Richard's throat. She smiles as his lifeblood jets and gurgles, soaking her faded dress and darkening the chill brine at her feet. She laughs and brandishes the knife on high, before tossing it out into the waves.

It is done and we are free...!

Triumphant, Sarah looks over at her lover and Daniel smiles back as he takes her hand.

Retribution—a life for a life. Inevitable.

* * *

Dawn paled the horizon, as the two of them dragged Richard's limp body up to the edge of a jagged rock. Tony gripped the dead man by his belt, and shoved. He pushed hard, sending Richard's corpse on his way. Together they watched Richard tumble and flop, as the wind whipped frenziedly in their faces. Exultant, Kate smiled as her husband's broken body vanished in the bitter wash below.

"We must make it look like an accident," Kate had told Tony, after she had sliced the knife into Richard's throat. "The locals knew what an idiot he was—no one will suspect any foul play, particularly when the sea's rotted his identity away." Tony had agreed readily, and so the two of them had dragged poor dead Richard up the steep face of a nearby rock, before casting him down into the water from on high.

Chapter 14

Maid of Haven

IT WAS A FISHERMAN FOUND Richard's headless body three days later. In the reception at Haven Hotel, the shaken girl Morwenna told the two kind policemen all she knew concerning the young couple from 'up country.' When they'd asked her about Mr. Harrison, Morwenna had shrugged.

"Nice enough, 'spose... bit odd... couldn't work him out really. Shame," she said shuddering, "—no one deserves that, do they?"

The deceased's wife Mrs. Katherine Harrison—who Morwenna informed the police was a bit snotty—had waited for Mr. Harrison's best friend to arrive and comfort her. This Tony Flannigan was some big-shot in the motor trade, apparently. It had been he that had spoken to the police, on account of Mrs. Harrison being too distraught. But to Morwenna there was something not quite right about those two.

"I wonder...?" she had thought back then.

But then, as winter wore on Morwenna soon forgot—she had the hotel to run, and little time to dwell on fancies. That said, there were other people in the parish a deal sharper than Miss Morwenna Hosking.

* * *

Kate was devastated of course—so Tony told the young officer and grey-haired sergeant. She'd no idea Richard had been contemplating suicide. How could she have? The guy had been through a rough patch, Tony explained. Some people grit their teeth and move on, but poor Richard had always been prone to moping. He was a bloody good bloke, Tony told them. The police had scratched their heads, and yawned agreement.

"We may need to question you again, sir,"—so the sergeant said. "But for now you're free to return to London. Look after his wife—won't you."

"Don't worry—I'll see she gets through this." Tony almost smiled then.

* * *

Later that morning as Kate Harrison packed the car, she awarded the ocean one last glance. It was dry but very cold, though the wind had finally eased. Kate shivered and turned away.

She checked herself, noticing a woman standing over by that distant rock. She was tall, her long, reddish hair dishevelled, and her face hidden from view. The woman was oddly familiar, though Kate couldn't recall where she had seen her before. She stood watching the breakers smash on the rocks—her apparel was little suited to the weather, and Kate wondered if she were unhinged. The strange woman seemed lost to time and space. Kate shrugged and turned away. It was time to leave this place at last—she and Tony had a life to live—again.

* * *

Spiral within a spiral: shifting sands and passing cloud. Moon and sun and driving rain—and still she waits.

And still she watches—the lonely maiden. She sees the blonde woman leave in her car, with her sleazy lover following eagerly behind. She sees through their disguise—witnesses the lost souls of Sarah and Daniel again reunited in their new earthly forms.

But this is not strange to her that sees everything. There is no mystery here—not for her. The sea claimed her own sweet love

long years ago—long before Richard and Kate and Tony, even before Sarah and Daniel and Thomas. For three hundred years, the
lonely maid of Haven has waited for her own love to return from
the depths of that cruel watery expanse. Time passes. Souls come
and go. She sees them all: the lost, the drowned, the starved and
the broken.

'From Hartland point to Padstow light, a ship's graveyard
by day and night'

* * *

So many souls lost to those cruel waves... For her the beach
is noisy—filled with their plaintive calls. Crowded and choking—
as such places often are by those trapped between two worlds.
Creatures of the void, they return to the ocean when day lightens
sky.

She alone remains constant and loyal to her duty. As of course
she must. But he has not returned (her only love,) and so, solitaire,
she must wait upon the next tide—her silent vigil continuing, until
the circle dance releases him again. As one day it surely must. And
so the Maid of Haven waits...

Epilogue

TONY FLANNIGAN READ KATE'S TEXT with one eye, while the other studied the road.

'Tired—can we pull over?'

Moments later, he moored up alongside Kate's Jimny. It was late, and drizzle murked the night.

They were somewhere on the A303—Somerset? Or maybe Wiltshire? God alone knew for sure. Kate looked shattered, so Tony suggested a proper sleep. The Travelodge they found was empty and forlorn. They paid for the room, and settled for the rest of the night, both far too tired for any thought of play.

Restless despite their fatigue, the lovers watched a movie and shared the bottle of claret Tony had picked up back at the garage. At 02.30 they clambered into bed. Tony snored, but Kate's mind was buzzing.

Something was wrong—but how could that be? They had been so thorough, and those policemen hadn't suspected a thing. Why would they? No, she was just overwrought.

And yet...?

Kate woke with a start—she must have slipped off, but was sure she hadn't slept for long. She shivered: strange how the room felt so cold, these places were normally very stuffy. Beside her, Tony still snored industriously. Kate's tired gaze strayed to the window, where the yellow light of the shabby lamp cast wan shadows on the wall.

A man sat there, watching her in silence. Kate's mouth dropped wide open.

Richard...?

Thomas smiled then:

"Sarah Hosking—did you really think you could get away from me?"

* * *

finis

A Note from the Author

Mostly I write fantasy. My new series Legends of Ansu is a heady blend of myth and mayhem—an ongoing opera of swordplay pitched to capture the middle ground betwixt the noble majesty of JRRT and the gritty realism of GRRM.

Not so with *The Haven*. This brief yarn was spun from entirely different thread. It's voice comes from my deep love and passion for Cornwall. For those of you that don't know it, Cornwall is where King Arthur was born—they do say—it's the sticky out bit at the South Western tip of jolly old England and known for shipwrecks, pirates and, much more recently, good ale, surfers and holiday folk. The county's wild coastline boasts some of the finest cliffs in the world whereas the stone clustered villages and copse-hidden churches hint at a time gone by.

I was fortunate to live in North Cornwall for many years. My late wife, Rae, was Irish and her love of that wild coast led us to settle halfway between her home and my own. Cornwall shares much in common with Ireland. Bude is nearer to Cork than London—in soul as well as miles, though the Celtic Sea separates them. In *The Haven* I have tried to hint at that connection. The Celtic Spirit is strongest close to the ocean.

Rae had that spirit. It is something that can be seen in her watercolours, two of these Maid of Haven and Anwynn, were the main inspiration and instigation for *The Haven* finding its words. Rae loved haunting tales though she never read *The Haven*—we lost her to cancer in late 2012. But I always promised her a ghost story so here it is. Rae's work can be viewed on her website www. Dizzardart.com or via the link in mine legendsofansu.com

Thank you for reading *The Haven*. I do hope that you enjoyed it. But take care if you wander the beach alone at night beneath that mischievous moon—Sarah and Daniel may not be out there, but you never know who is...

~JWW 2014

Subscribe to my weekly newsletter at
legendsofansu.com

Please review this novel — always nice to know
what my readers think.

Thank you and enjoy!
J.W. Webb